MAL

# POETIC
# RAMBLINGS
—— OF A ——
# DISENCHANTED
# SOUL

## DANNY WARREN

authorHOUSE®

*AuthorHouse*™ UK
*1663 Liberty Drive*
*Bloomington, IN 47403 USA*
*www.authorhouse.co.uk*
*Phone: 0800.197.4150*

*Published by AuthorHouse 03/20/2017*

*ISBN: 978-1-5246-7909-5 (sc)*
*ISBN: 978-1-5246-7910-1 (hc)*
*ISBN: 978-1-5246-7911-8 (e)*

*Print information available on the last page.*

# CONTENTS

# A LAST SLEEP

Darkness is the comforter of the coward
In his desperate pursuit of one more lie.
Gateways to helplessness
Yawn their invitations
To destitution and regret
In the tranquil balm
That is nocturnal oblivion.
Yet still I wait in expectations,
Real or unreal,
For the word that will finally announce transcendence
To this waif trapped in the miseries
Of illusion and imperfection.
Smiles and light are so life
In the longing which is existence,
Littered with rewards gloomily greeted
As if everyday gifts were monotony
In survival's necessary requirement
For the function of an endless sleep.
Waking dormant permanence
Is the legacy of this impromptu eternity,
Where time will always be the liar
In the interlink of lives
And promised absolution.
So again I must awake
And smile at the song,
Struggling to recall the relevance of words
Whose importance whispers through the wastage
Of countless tempting dreams
To a sleep that will finally last!

# AFTERMATH

I bare my pain
And languish in my misery and loss.
Your flowers are my flowers
In the perpetual severance
Of all our memories and joys.
Darkness envelops my consciousness,
Blanking out all sensation
Save my need to hold you.
Tears weave a sinuous deliberation
Of wanton melancholy,
Carving a path etched by repetition-
Wasted dejected eyes.
All I can give you is my silence
And my outstretched heart.
Let it sustain you
Until we are together again.

# AGE-OLD AGE

Rusting rhythms hum their sad songs
In a world of newer dreams
Dedicated to the last stone
Thrown into a ringing stream.

Memories of aches and places;
Sympathies of stranger times
Unrecorded with the smiles
Of expectations other rhymes.

Dangerous and optimistic
Hopes in plenty show the way.
Age, with all its wild progressions,
Keeps the world of death at bay.

Distances are but a whisper,
Little left to want and grieve.
Lifetime sake and lifetime ending,
Aged insensitivity.

# AIRSHIP

Silence hums to a drifting void
Breath'd by hints of air
Born in the gasp of timeless memory,
Serene in its solitude.
Led like some fortunate mariner
Through mountainous billows of grace and form.
Icebergs arch into the sky,
Stately, delicate,
Declaring their grandeur.
So we become together in companionship,
In mutual contemplation,
Feeling oh so gently,
As though a careless touch might yet warm
This alien eye.
Blessed calmness assails senses,
Pleading for the familiar perceptions
Of a painful Earth.
Solidity, transient, reluctant
Parts for an embrace and a welcome
With the delicacy of air,
Sealing us in its absorption
With a final caress of absolution.
I used to think I knew you,
World of worlds,
Intensity becalmed with the sweetness
Of final isolation.
Yet now I gaze
In grateful wonderment,
For all the world like a God,
At the magnificence of it all.

DANNY WARREN

# ALTAR BOYS

Incense sweating,
Altar dressing
Brassed and pompous,
Shining homage.
All I feel is supplication,
Morning mass or benediction,
Upright standards in precision.
Three a side in fair division,
Recall one more moment when
I come in prayer to see again
Your tabernacled sentinels
Upstanding, unashamed.

# HELLO, GOODBYE

Where are you staying, my darling?
You're not in the same place as me.
I see in your distant reflections
The glazed look of your mysteries.

I so want a share of your silence,
To know if you're lost and in pain.
To see if the secrecy within yourself
Is part of a different refrain.

And how long ago was it, darling,
You seemed not to recognise me:
It seems such a long time ago now;
You acted irrationally.

And how much I weep at your actions;
You're so unaware of my pain.
You just don't know how, and you just don't know why;
Still you do it again and again.

I'm so sad; I know it's all over.
You don't see my face anymore.
This dreadful affliction that Alzheimer named
Has finally closed your mind's door.

And yet, in your quiet situation,
You still have the key to my heart.
Perhaps in your strange, distant, new netherworld,
You still know that we'll never part.

# AMBITION

Again, you greet me,
Awakening as a somnolent flower,
Disgorging optimism
And radiant expectation:
One more new day.

Time and effort,
Motivation, stimulus, and greed
Demand the best
That I can give:
That I will make my way
Come desperation.

And vague memorials,
Pathways etched in stone
Of failures past and gone,
Will be the guide
That steers me ever onward
To journey's end.

# DEAR ANGEL

I never ever met you – or perhaps I did
In a long-ago sleep,
Inspiring all my painful longings,
Fading with the abruptness of an unfinished whisper
In another desiccated dawn.
Investing a linger like the ache of lost perceptions;
An unsustainable memory that leaves only pain
And melancholy to remember you by.
I tell myself that we'll meet again one day,
In another time that will transpose itself into a new dream state
Where instants of real disappointment
Are just the foretaste of a better tomorrow,
And you will be my reality forever.
Am I allowed these confusions
In the selection of my moments
And the times that I can enjoy them in
When presences and pleasures are as real to me
As the scents that time strews
Through the essences of my imagination
And my existence?
My best measures are in the care, which is part of me,
With me,
Watching me,
And being the very best that I can imagine,
Ever present in this waking dream.

# 911 SWANSONG

Betrayed by wretchedness and bated breath
Do throes of end day founder in farewells
At all the miseries impressed beneath
This ruined heart wherein misfortune dwells.

And tears and fortitude plead for recourse
To lost and found subjection to a time
So carelessly commanded and endorsed
As real achievement in this world of crime.

Yet whisper loud your gestures with appeal,
And cry but secretly your devil's name
That all who heed his sorcery may kneel
In meek subjection to this day of shame.

But greatness lies in wishing for some part
Of one more chance to heal this broken heart.

# GARDENER AT ARROMANCHE

Expansive, disparate symmetry
Fawns at the day with familiar pains,
A swathe of tears upon this shroud of death,
Meadow of ephemeral hospitality.
Quiet submissions defy the whispers
That utter wherever stones
Share the gentle breaths,
The briefest murmurs
That are the saddest exchanges
Of their lost tales and memories.
And what do you hear
With your own mask of recollections
As you ply your solitary dedication
Through these desolated rows of indignant waste,
Preening and combing
Their secrets and stories
That they, at the very least, deserve to have saved
From the mishaps of their abbreviated existences?
Pause at a name,
A time, a memory
You knew or know or might have known
Out of the histories which are the souls
In this unhappy place.

# ARTISTIC FIX

Joy of liberty
Tempts fear and pain,
Expressions of the heart,
Eager substance for a pen
Weighted with deliverance.
If truth hangs heavily
With the doubts and hesitations
Of a less than happy spirit,
How much more difficult can it be
When sad conviction
Only offers the certainty
That an open heart
Retains the curiosity
Of its own dilemma?
Personal structure of experience,
A pain shared
Serves to enhance
The misery of sad recollection
In others
By rekindling memories
Best forgotten.
True poetry must be truthful,
Or it fails in the mire
Of its own hypocrisy.
Artistic persistence,
Even at the risk of misunderstanding,
Is important if there is something to say,
So say it well
Or unsay go away!

# BAD

It's certainty the worst word I will ever learn
That I'm supposed to understand the meaning of.
How soon should I begin to really know a sin,
Equating it to every action ever done,

Or saw, or thought, or badly enough wanted
That might be vaguely construed as unclean
By my controllers, often self-appointed,
With disconcerting, barely concealed glee?

"Too bad!" became in very shortened order
The object of life's stipulation stone.
Bad boys, bad girls, bad food, bad everything
You never, ever want to bring back home.

To Mummy and to Daddy for inspection
And comforting smiles, surreptitious glows
Of condescending, righteous approval—
The sort of good thing every parent knows.

Yet bad has become pretty rife with day and age,
With bigger, better, bad things all the rage.
It's even become hip to become badder
Than all the badder people up the stage.

Yeah! Bad is good now, like a false affliction.
A readiness for comfort and a plea
For all those childhood threats and posturings
To just leave me alone and let me be.

# BANKRUPT

Laughter lies like a bedraggled swansong
In eyes where faith is glazed by new-found fears.
Unsaid admissions shattered like a penance,
Or so it seems, for unremembered years.

In darkness, comfort dwells, a gentle thief,
Conditioned subterfuge of septic calm
For doubtful mind to drift and dwell beneath.
Deceptive absolutions, free from harm.

And yet harsh realisms play and bloom
With whispers of insidious intent,
While mischief moments perpetrate a gloom
Of misery and sorrow and regret.

Oh, folly of possession, make me be
Achievement-savoured spiritually.

# MALDON BARGE RACE

Forested castles, stately, serene.
Dowager passaged, voluptuous beamed.
Glorious, grandiose, breathless of air,
Tranquil, mysterious, devil may care.

Signalling readiness, billow, uncurl,
Pupescent chrysalis image unfurls.
Watching as they saunter languidly by,
The waiting crowd cheers, and the gulls swoop and cry.

Carnival-spirited sunshine and smiles,
Sun-struck pedestrians seeking for miles,
Stroll on the promenade, gazing away,
Mastheads receding: a glorious day.

Emptiness, misery, now that they've gone,
Fine upright megaliths sailing for fun.
Will we see them again, know where they've been?
Never a race this one, more of a scene.

# DEAR BEN

Months pass;
Deceptive lies
That promised a better tomorrow
Tempered with time.

Betrayal lives
In the last long look
Of eyes that sought to understand
That everything was still the same
In the distance.

Tragic truth:
Knowledge that total loyalty
And trust
Were rewarded in the end
By desertion.

Desolation:
Awareness of ultimate failure,
Pain at how easily dispensed
Was someone who cared
So deeply for me.

Tremulous time,
Home of meetings
Flavoured with accidents
Of unexpected affection
Live on for me.

# BESTSELLERS

Number one bestsellers seem like two-a-penny dreadfuls:
Buy it if you dare; there'll be another right behind.
Take your time in choosing it, if you have time to spare
To see if rhyme and reason lurk within the lines.


Languish in the misdemeanours of some sordid theme
Laced with relish on the platter of a dream.
Find your life reflected in the image in the strands
Gently filtering through mystic super schemes.


Live the expectations of the packaging and print
And the promise of some scrumptious delight,
Cast in stone and offered as the prelude to the feast
Cased within each tasteful page in black and white.


Disinter a heartbeat as the multifolded sights
Of a thousand helpless moments are proposed,
Naked and forever in a tale of cryptic blame
With the reader and the writer juxtaposed.

# BIRTH, UNBIRTHED

I am the endless alchemy of breathless needs
Entreating with the nervousness of hungry greeds;
Predacious expectations mouthed in mindless glees
Beg absolution for the very best that used to be.

Birthday breasted bare indulgences repast,
Serve all illusions of existence meant to last
Into eternity for goodness' sake and goodness' past;
And who would have it otherwise when dies are cast.

Until brave adolescence teaches greater sins
Of timeless retribution on survivals wings,
Decision time is not the comforter that hymns
Proclaim as goodness in a world where evil wins.

For truth is always casualty when might or slight
Sees envy and intolerance as black and white.
In worldly ways compassion's needs are only right
When native expectations lead into the light.

# Birthday Boy

To look through watered eyes to watered eyes,
Tears of pleasure prize, tears of surprise
Follow in my nakedness and my despair:
In closeness and in warmth against this frightful air.


Are longing or desire the only friends I feel—
Terrified, awakened chitter chatter glees?
Hands that hardly hug embracing gentle fear,
Clasping tender eyes that seek so deep so near.

# BLACK AND WHITE

Did I appease your monochrome insistence,
  Absorb your philanthropic masquerades
  Of flaccid gratitude and stilted promises
Consistent with your normal days to days?

  Your regulation orders without question,
  Impressed in habit of the starkest form
  Perverted liberties and imperfections—
    A stultifying mirage of the norm?

So have I suffered from your stark precisions,
Impressed in dogmas sharp as black and white
  And read all over, prayerful intermissions
Of faith inlaid with shame and guilt and fright.

  Your pictures in my mind are pain to me,
    As smiles and sadness visit equally.

# Blind Estate

Comforted in glazed seclusion,
Light lays its warmth
To his unrelenting measure.
His visionary chords are life
In his stall of tactile memories.
Air wafts in and out of idled lips,
Rhythmic reminders of the weaknesses
Of continuation.
In this hush of existence,
Audio-visual diversions,
Cursed with the pain of repetition,
Fade into recent memory,
And dark silence hangs like a pall
In this void of colourless obscurity.
A tentative hand extends,
Seeking touching recognition
In a glass placed with other
Comfortable familiars.
Sightless eyes in empty resignation
Lie in a sink of opaque secrecy,
Intent on some prefabricated world
Made favourite with time.

# BOOK

We are both so much older.
Do I still smell as good to you?
Your fingers so caressing:
Delighting in pleasures new.

I am resurrection and life.
I am divinity clouded by illusions
And misconceptions.
My name is my plea,
And my word is my being.

Breathe-life is in me
As the wisps of secrecy
On drifted pages
Give new life to you.
Partake of me in this communion,
And I will live forever.

Now you want to silence me!
Cook me up a little!
You see me as big-headed
When you're just afraid of me.

I could help, you know,
If only you'd let me!
Don't fear a truth
That won't be changed
Or diluted
By your anger.

Look at me now,
This heap of ash.
Do I still smell as good to you
As you toy with your wisdoms?

You think
You can extinguish truth
By extinguishing me.
My truth will persist.
I am still resurrection and life,
And I will be here
Long after you have gone.

# BOUDICCA

Do you believe in glory
In your madness and your pain?
Solitude and sympathy
Remain your only friend.

Trust in life naivety
Is poor as bitter wine
When sipped in Roman fellowship
And hope of better times.

Foolish Prasutagus,
In his wisdom and his thought,
Bespoke the need for peace in time
And possible reward.

And Nero, how he must have smiled
His gracious evil whim,
That imbecile barbarians
Should seek to trust in him.

Despatched he in unduly haste
His loyal legion hordes
To quell with all sincerity
The brave Iceni swords.

Ah! Boudicca, how well you fought
And who is there to say
That warriors so brave and coarse
Will ever rue that day?

With courage and with recklessness,
With curses and with rage,
Did Iceni and Roman blood
Flow freely on this stage.

So many cried, so many died
In feeding Roman whims.
What sadness are the tears that taste
The bitterness within.

And names are time and legacy,
And courage pastures sweet,
That needs the bravery of death
To make such names complete.

# CANCER IMPATIENT

Futures seem a distant glimmer
In eyes wearied by tearful resignation;
Fanciful plans talking about tomorrows
Coerced by the doubtful viewpoint
Of a nervous insecurity.
Dreams become a fleck of memory
In the miseries which are stooping agony
And shameful helplessness.
All I see in you is a past, which has gone forever.
All I want is a future
Which embraces some part
Of knowledge that always included you.
The coughing begins again,
And the mists of foolish optimism
Are dissipated in the racking convulsions
Which never want to end
Once they have started to feed.
I try to watch then look away, coward that I am;
My absolution cannot include the gasps of your agony—
So agonied!
Sleep, that traitorous friend,
Spreads its secret blanket
To work what silent mysteries it may
Beneath the lives of us all,
And the smiles and tears, which are the fragments of its nether world,
Still carry in their grasp
The final solutions to so many of the questions
About this life that we don't dare to ask.

# CHAIN-LINK

Come and walk with me among the flowers,
And drink the earthen fragrance
Lost for frantic need
Of dark, misguided alchemies
And greeds.
Confusing dream conceits
Are transient as spindrift,
Disguising real necessities,
Feeding existence
With the mistaken ideology
Of a drug-crazed need,
Formed and fermented
In confused minds
Till all there is
Is the desperation
For one more material fix.
So spare me the promises
Of chain-link destinies
In this time-worn travesty
Of multicoloured hologram
Fixations.
My dreams will dream on
With the infantile precision
That eternal hope requires.
The passionate optimism
Of memory,
Even tarnished by incessant betrayals,
Will prevail in the end
With substance intact.
Fervent belief

DANNY WARREN

That truth is the ultimate weapon
Meshes well
With the abiding conviction
That good and bad
Will always be linked
In this interchange of life.

# CHALLENGE

What dreams and memories
Are etched into this vanity
Of misconception
And disillusionment?
The promises of childhood fantasies
Drift away with the years,
Until all that remains
Are the dusts of an ambition
Stultified by the disaffections
Of innumerable betrayals.
In my grown-up disguises,
I live with the disabilities
That helping hands
Have made me feel comfortable with
For comfort's sake.
I see myself with the disguises
That life pleases to call challenges,
Wearing them to myself
In my nakedness.
I watch excuses floating by
With the inconsistency of familiar comfort,
Waiting to prop up the next failure.
I see all the times that I have tried to be right,
And I think there might still be a success
In this game of life swansong.

# CHESS MASTERS

With idle gaze unerring, play is cast
And battle joined unsynchronised aboard
Of matadors at honour-bound impasse,
To quell with give and guile the static horde.

In reverence, countless silent gods implore
Their champions in their name to entertain,
With subtlety oblique and mental claw,
The fall of fellow's household and of king.

And so does move and counter cut and swathe
With affable extinction to and fro
To plaudits mutely tangible and grave
Of fascinations praying afterglow.

So is infamy's practical design:
A tranquil, silent, validated crime.

# CHILDHOOD'S END

You lies of mine, you permeated
All my conscious thoughts.
Those childhood inconsistencies
Bespoke the dreams they brought.
Those never-ending, ever-blending
Erstwhile fantasies
Pretended to bequeath to me
A kind reality.


Safe, sheltered, and cocooned
From life's harsh inequalities,
The playthings of my consciousness
Gave me the life I pleased:
Substantial and rewarding
As reality then seemed,
Sad confrontations left me doubting
Pleasantries and schemes.


Ah, gentle friend, I trusted you.
I lived within your truth
And watched the flower of ignorance,
Uncultivated youth,
Reach blindly for that virgin day
When all would be revealed
And all those wounds of childhoods past
Will finally be healed.

# CHILDREN OF GOD (LAMENT)

Ah! Children of My heart, My love, My life, My bitterness!
I see you in My wake and in My dream, such tenderness
Misled in Me these visions of perfection and distress:
Misguided arrogance of man, such damned omnipotence!


In loving you, forsaking all I hold as dear and true,
Rare tolerance and passion – nay, forgiveness am I due.
Such anger raves illogic in the search for some lost truth
And nestling in this heart of God, the search for one lost youth.


Ah! Foolish time, you lie to Me, you teach and then you sin.
These travesties of virtue all committed with a grin
Till life and all its absolutions finally wear thin.
And yet! And yet – My breaking heart – you will not let Me in!

# CHOICES

Give me a gun; I'll give you peace.
Give me a child; I'll make him mine.
Give me a bomb; I'll help you pray
For me before you watch me die.


Give me a word I can understand.
Give me a smile to fit my crime.
Give me a soul that I might see
My silent tears at burial time.


Give me a flower and let it grow.
Give me a book and read to me.
Give me a breath and let it be
My dying breath in history.


Give me an eye and pain to see.
Give me the world at break of dawn.
Give me peace enough to leave
The bomb and gun and pain alone.

# COEXISTENCE

Fabric society,
Tolerance with space,
Strangers and bedfellows,
Nervous embrace.

Respect for kinship,
Come join the play.
Starts as it ends
In a personal way.

Law and disorder,
Taken in turns,
Argue and walk away,
Fighting to learn.

Comfort and unity,
Family and friends,
Shaken up and disturbed—
Mischievous blends.

Working relationships
Flavoured with time,
Kind fabrications
Our gentlest crime.

Smile at a distance,
Tentative hands
Hold on to secrets
I understand.

# The Comet

I saw a comet the other day,
And as I looked, it went away.
I don't know if it's tricking me;
It flew too far for me to see.

I wonder why there's so much fuss
At something with a tail of dust.
Mummy says it hasn't gone,
But just keeps flying on and on.

I'll have a look again tonight,
Just to see if Mummy's right,
Or if that glow in front of me
Is where it fell into the sea.

DANNY WARREN

# CONVENT

How dare you!
I own you,
Control you,
Dare you!

Take this pain,
This anger,
This fear.
Feel this fear.

Shrouded spectres
Black.
Why black
And blue?

What pain
And sadness.
I will have your pain,
Your tears,
Your truth,
The better
To batter you.

How dare you
Dare me
With thought!

# THE CRYING GAME

At all the world he poses,
Slouched in oblivious content,
Smiling secretly at some private joke,
Encased in a distant memory.
The spent blanket clings desperately
To shoulders stooped in the dregs
Of a final last laugh.
Nervously a droplet trembles,
And I lean across to chase it away;
It won't be the last.
I wonder if he feels the cold.
I wonder if he feels.
The cold is in the walls,
Carrying eyes in their shadows—
Eyes that bear the last lines
Of condemnation and defeat
In the leaded silence.
Sound weighs heavily in the gloom,
Sterilised solitude of distances
That only serve to insist that life really does exist
Beyond these hollowy halls.
I watch the carers as they stare desperately ahead,
Hurrying past
For fear they might yet be caught out
When the music finally ends.

# DEAD LEAVES

Don't talk to me of dead leaves in the twilight of my years,
When all I have are golden rays of comfort for my tears
And smiles at all the memories of friends I used to see
In twilights that are clearer than this vague acrimony.

As new o'clock recurring doubts intrude on each new day,
Awakening anew those wasting promises that play;
As fading faces in some fading, friendless, empty room,
Misty-eyed uncertainties that crowd the breaking gloom.

So dead these leaves that falter in their desperate decline,
Insensitive to all the different elements of time
Like life and love and smiles and caring thoughts for what-have-beens:
Regenerating memories as leafless evergreens.

# DEAR RESURRECTION

Stay a while, I pray,
Where mutual misconceptions make you real for me,
And all your pain
Still feeds my selfish need for sweet reality.
And yet I see
Within your eyes a longing need to be
Adrift in dear,
Ecstatic, painless liberty.

It's such a shame:
Our precious love so rare and true through all these years—
Or so it seems—
Was squandered on illusions of dear might-have-beens.
The fantasies we shared
Were prepossessive thoughts, true love soliloquies.
And now regretful tears
Are all I have to comfort me.

Farewell, dear heart.
My joys and cares will stay with you through endless time,
And when our days
Collide again in mutual eternity,
Then we will be
In some vast, coexistent, loving grace
As one again
In pure, convergent, spaced tranquillity.

# Diana – In Memoriam

Classless ignominy, still
You mock my helplessness.
Sad vanity, breeding feeds
On my impotent bitterness.

My life and loves and feelings
Leave me wistfully aware
Of some dissatisfactions,
Great ambitions left impaired.

Ah, joy! How much I miss you,
Multifaceted disguise,
As smiling caution shows its face
In your imploring eyes.

Yet in my tears and trials,
In my days of cruel deceit—
Ah, yet! The day bears fruit
For me in failures so complete.

# DYSFUNCTION

Memory hurts the most:
The indifference and fun of youth.
Olduns never figured
In my scheme of things,
Except when they had to be avoided
Or waited for.
Frail hands,
Wrinkled and sore,
Twisted and arthritic,
Draw the pen
With testy, jerky strokes.
Blurred eyes strain,
Needing to see
(And failing)
With straining tears
And pain.
Nothing works
As it used to.
Everything is time
And effort,
And I can only grin
At the humility
And pain
Of it all.

# Don't Look Back in Anger

Dream on, dear friend,
For distant recollections are your history,
And all the joys of erstwhile flavoured imagery
That visit you in waking and in sleeping
Will comfort you,
And time will be the sweeter in their keeping.
And smile a while,
Embrace the secrets, colour laughter memories
That flicker by as unlost, unreal subjects,
True soliloquy.
And tend your days
In peaceful abstinence of painful truth,
So guiding you through tranquil dream meanderings
Of long-lost youth.
And never say that all was pointless nothingness
So long ago,
For all you are
Are myriad reflections of your afterglow;
And time will play
Your nurtured, self-elusive, comfort rainbow end
At all the happiness this life has brought
For you, dear friend.

# DREAM STATE

Such painful wakingness
Such disappointment
Such longing loss
Such missingness of joy
Such memory of tenderness eternal
Such loving looking sharingness of soul
Such pain of truth so mystically secret
Such kindness intertwined in hands of gold
Such smiling eyes in mine in life eternal
Such quiet pleasure magical and real
Such joy of conversation, tranquil, silent
Such fantasy and folly memory
And pain of pain, oh, how I miss that being
Save that it brought me closer still to you

# DREAMSCAPE

Am I on a travel homeward,
Home to where the seas are real?
Dreams admonish silence dearly,
Deathly as the whispers steal
On the shades of mystery as
Wavelets splash in idle play:
Gentle billows overhead
Help lazy times to drift away.

Otherworldly, deep reflections
Shining through the fading calm:
Shimmering in invitation,
Secret songs that beg me come
Helplessly towards the finite,
Floating tenderly away,
Solitude, endearing friend
Ship; still I see you, still I pray.

In your welcome do I know you,
Though you never have a name:
Comfortable in your smiling
Being and your calm refrains:
Easing gently to the motions
Of the lull that leads your feet
To the milk of make-believe
While leading me away to sleep.

# DSO

So this is it then?
This is what all the fuss and folly
Was for, at the end of the day?
I used to think I knew;
Now I just think.
Hiding behind this beige bravado,
I temper my perceptions
With brave words
And silences.
Gazing philosophically
At this crutch among my crutches,
Sporting a heroism
Which only seems starker today
For the futility
That it engenders:
What a tableau of hopelessness
We fools presented,
Trapped in a past whose shadow
Is the only promise
Of existence,
Still seeking answers
Which refuse to come easily.
At least you come back to me
With your terrors and your secrets:
Same, and not the same.
Memories of pain and parting
Fading in and out
As the fear and imprecision

DANNY WARREN

Which made all this possible
In the first place seeps away.
All I have now is memory,
But all I feel is you,
And that must be enough for me,
Till I forget!

# EARTHSONG

Allow me some indulgences, if you will,
When I say that nothing is enough anymore:
Cold, warm,
Chilled, awake,
Feeling the fidgets of a restless earth.
I have to say that I'm not always ready for this new clamour,
This exuberance of determined regeneration.
I know all about need and must and all that sort of thing, but really
The patter of tiny feet at the first signs of change
Have become just a little too repetitive for my taste.
And then it's want, want, want; take, take, take.
It just keeps on coming, and I just keep turning it out!
Well, it can't go on indefinitely.
Tiring, aching,
I yearn to sleep—
Not your year-after-year kind as life starts to cool down sleep,
But real, holding-back sleep without all this anticipation,
Couched in the somnolence of beautiful inactivity,
Bathed in the folds of a carpet of brown and cold,
To shake indifference at the prospect of a cancelled spring.
Wouldn't that be a sleep we would all remember,
Not like ever after sleep lasting only so long as memory permits,
But real sleep that will fade into the yearnings of ultimate regret?
So share your stop with mine, if you wish,
And lapse into the comfort of a sublime winter
That will go on forever.
It could be the infinite discovery, for you as well as for me,
As we share the longings of all those might-have-beens
Finally lapsing into the embrace of a bedtime,
Laughing together at this last long joke.

DANNY WARREN

# ETERNITY THROUGH A CHILD'S EYES

What is this place where madness dwells,
This void of endless nothingness?
No dear distractions venture in;
No light dares kiss the dark abyss.

Despair is life within the depths
Of awful fascination dreams.
Oh! Soul of man, you live in pain
And timelessness exists unseen.

You depth of ancient mystery,
You secrecy of hidden face:
What answers, what transparencies
Are living in your deep embrace?

Ah, death, I cannot look at you
With fearless eyes that gaze within,
The isolation you embrace
Where terror is my final sin.

# FANTASTIC FANTASIA

Fantasia fantastical,
Glorious spectrally,
Extravagance sur spa,
Maldon, you grew for me.

Welcome the lowing skies,
Sing with the bands,
Ooh! Audiovisual
Thunderclap sounds.

Watery symphonies,
Fountains of youth,
Hasten nostalgia
With seventies truth.

Exploding starbursts,
Lazerly lights,
Skylight crescendo—
Such wonderful sights.

And then it's all over,
And evening is done;
'Twas more than I came for,
Such riotous fun!

# FEAR

I know you,
You tenuous reflection
Of memories that drift
Vague as a dream.
Far removed from today
In time and space,
The swathe of childhood recollections
Are the ghosts of pains
That haunt the waking years
Like repressive nightmares:
And so I know you,
Yet I know you not!

Shall I thank you all
For your secrecies,
Your cosseting deceptions
Disguised as care in fear's name?
Warnings of dire retribution
Were fears I would know your fear:
When I hesitate to answer,
I know you have taught me well.
Yes, they knew you too,
Yet they knew you not!

And will I laugh at you
When waking demise
Finally lifts its veil
On this illusion.
Will I wake and wonder
At the misgivings and hesitations,

The wasted opportunities,
And know that you acted
In my best interests
For fear of harming me?
Oh, yes! I'll know you then,
With all your bare decisions
And your shame.

# FEASTER

Oh! Gift of life and death and death and timeless sin,
What succour dear redeemer do you share?
This mortal folly that we suffer in:
This tragedy of ignorance laid bare.

Yet here we lie and cheat and name our price
With Godly Mammon, real yet so surreal:
Still do we honour your great sacrifice!
Behold the heathen egg and hearty meal.

In recollection of Your final days,
We play with wisdom, holiday with flair.
What truthful moral virtue fills your gaze?
This fast existence worshipped everywhere.

Ah, life! You blessed punishment, embrace.
My sin, remain my friend, my life, my faith.

# FINAL SLEEP

Everything changes in sleep:
Oblivion welcomed as a lie
Told too many times to disguise the pain
Of new truths that will heal all
If we choose them to.

Testaments of desire,
Comforters that protect concepts of sanity
That we may bask on the altar of egos
While sleeping the sleep of the fool
When we choose to.

Yes I see all in sleep,
Failures and pleasures,
The reality of a dream time which only ends
In the eternity, which is the waking,
And finally there are no choices.

# First Sin

Thanks for the memory.
The knock-on effect
Of original desire
Haunts my existence
Like the unwelcome legacy
Of some perverse
Genetic instability.
And don't talk to me
About free will—
As if predestination
Equates to some misguided concept
Of a level playing field.
I know right,
And I know wrong,
And I know which is easier.
And I thank you for that.
It is, however, difficult
Labouring under the illusion
That my options
About whether to succumb
To temptations or not
Are still choices
That I make for myself.
It would be nice to know
That it hasn't all been for nothing
At the end of the day.
The eternal irony
Of this ultimate enigma
Will probably be with me
For as long as I draw breath.
As hand-me-down sins go,
It really is the pits.

# GOOD FORTUNE

Freeze-dried concepts, timeless energies
Spoken in the twinkling of a transcendental eye.
Gifted effervescence of a subliminal waking phrase
Blessed and spoken in splendid benevolence
For distribution to waking laughter.
Pain is not my weakness
In the glad distribution of this benediction.
Distant melancholies threaten all goodness
With violent references to familiarity
Tainted by the sweet greed that stains
All fortunate intervention.
Disaffection and longing are disparate bedfellows
In the headlong search for solutions
That will provide the answers
And satisfy them all at the same time.
Good fortune is like the spindrift
Of transient lifetime passages,
Reflecting the vagaries
Of singular expectations
So that the taste and aftertaste
Will always be different
As well.

# FOSSIL

Ages drift and sway
Within the mirage
Which is imagination.
Timelessness
Is handheld icons
Hinting at depths as infinite
As the joy song
Of discovery and speculation.
To wonder at the lies and promises
That bedevil you
Is to wish at mysteries
Which beckon with messages,
Shouting across the distances
And finding that no one is listening.

# FRIENDSHIP

I remember friendship—
Or was it just a dream,
Like the fun of childhood?

I remember hands that talked and fought,
Then learned to talk again
With tenuous touches.

I remember space,
And smiles at the silences,
And the promise of a new purpose.

I remember missing what I had,
Then ran off to something better—
Bitter better.

I remember believing that friendship would conquer all,
Except religious and racial bigotry.
And it always did.

I remember my friends,
Whose smiles across the years
Are the same as the glimpses
Of yesterday.

Mostly, though, I remember you,
And I never have to tell you
Why I do.

DANNY WARREN

# FUNERALS

Funerals are hidden faces
Bowed in hidden thoughts and hidden fears.
Funerals are memories
Of anger at the spoils of wasted years.
Funerals are smiles
Of recollections of a face from long ago.
Funerals are hellos and goodbyes
At strangers, wondering as they go.
Funerals are promise and regret,
And believing at the time.
Funerals are recriminations,
Pleasure's peach with soothing glass of wine.
Funerals are violent
Discharges in a world of violent peace.
Funerals are true regeneration,
Blessing laughter with release.

# FUNEREAL THOUGHT

Dream and discovery! Now it begins:
The sweetness of death and the silence of sin.
Do you still see me, and are you still here,
Rueing the wastage of mistier years?

Time, with its parodied pleasantry song,
Teases each moment as though it was one
With universe elements' need to perceive:
Chastening paradox, prism of greed.

Talk to me when I sleep; tell me it's so:
All you perceive in the world that you know.
The treasures of consequence yours to enjoy;
Feast of a greedy soul, eyes of a boy.

Care for this past in its timeless embrace:
That time set its stall in some happier place.

# Gardener

Seasons share their promises
Through dewy, lustred eyes.
Fond reminiscences lead gaunt hands
Over tracts of sublime familiarity,
Whispering at him through the verdant silence
Of eternal optimism.
Resurrection is the mystery of the day
For the children of this first gush
Of breathless emergence
At the hope of new life.
A thank-you that comes
From a gentle touch of care;
Encouragement begun with the caress
Of a practiced finger and thumb.

# GENESIS

Decide in your wisdom,
Deduction, seduction:
How it was meant to be
Counter-production.
All of it history;
Tell me you didn't know.
God in his heaven,
Satanic overthrow.
Pass me a bigger leaf:
Who's here with us?
Disrobed embarrassment,
Guilt-ridden fuss!

# GHOST CRY

Do you feel liberated?
Is purgatory's end
The blessed release
That sleep is made of?
What hurt was it that bound you to this time
Where fear of pain is the final arbiter
In the sorry process
That promises redemption
For believing long enough?

# GHOST

I see you
Engrossed in your dream state residue:
Here, yet not here,
Spiritual shadow paste,
Trail of a memory.
Do the walls hold your stories
And leak them just for me?
Your silence damns you,
Tormentor of souls
Adrift in ultimate ignorance,
Ultimate ambition,
Ultimate lifetime.
Yet I do see you—
But which of us is in the dream?

# GIFTS

Gifts I squandered foolishly
Came too late to furnish me.
Far too late for me to know
Chances that I had to grow.

Isn't this the way it works?
Just one more of lifetime's quirks:
Up and down and sink and shame;
Shrug, regret, and start again.

# THROUGH THE LOOKING GLASS DARKLY (1984)

I could so much have saved your futile deaths,
Had I the need to warn you of your folly
And your flippancies.
As things are, dear children, I forgive you
And bask in the lugubrious delights
Of your final subjugation.
Greet me as the spectre that has no name,
A number of the nightmare that haunts recollection
With the diligence of a terror tale
Fed to generations who believed and feared—
But only for a while!
I spy with my little eye;
Such a brittle eye is it, to be sure,
But it sees you all, my dears,
With the certainty that cynicism brings.
Shall I carry you screaming
On this helter-skelter which is life?
Will I laugh at your fears
And your wide-eyed panic mentions
At the sights which have no words,
But bring only lasting truths
Through lasting tears?

# GODHEAD

Suddenly time seems not to curry my favour:
Galaxies swing this way and that
In the interminable breeze,
Which is motion so discrete,
As to whisper its message in the language
Of timeless permanence.
I could find you, if I chose,
In the drifting permavoid of awful silences.
But I know you are here,
And I am all the thoughts,
Free and immeasurable,
That are the babble of one
And the whispers of us all.
Voices, so much smile and discretion,
Are comfortable with answers
That transcend the need to seek
Not because we know,
But because we no longer need to know.
We hear the questions:
Curse of sad mortality
In the intermingling of cosmic waves.
And you breathe our song
In your heady motion through our dreams
And your own existence.

# GOOD NIGHTSHIFT

You charming mystery of sweet content,
Come lay beside me, greet the waking morn.
Your kind embrace a welcoming expanse
Of weariness as pleasant as the dawn.

A lifting chatter, fertile, gently plays
Of eager songsters calling to the day,
Pervading dulled impressions, sleepy haze,
Like comfort resting, balmy, new mown hay.

A wafting breeze, soft, urges me awake
To hinting sunbeams warmth and scented air
And wistful breaths so charm this dreamlike state,
This tranquil moment rich with idle care.

Oh! Somnolence, what secrets do you know?
Is dawn's sweet call lost night-time's afterglow?

# GOODBYE, WORK

I will be so glad
When the machine finally spits me out
Like so much disposable detritus.
No longer to be demented
By fears of destitution,
Quavering to the needs of slavers
With constitutional deficiencies.
I will laugh with tearful disillusionment
At new liberties I will be able to engage
In ways that I have always imagined,
Savouring the madness.
Oh! For the freedom to believe the dreams,
To dispel all the doubts
That have made life that little bit less viable.
Can I have a little eccentricity in my present
And tell the world to go to hell,
At least until I become old enough
That I can join in it all
And not mind their laughter
Anymore?

# GOODBYES

I see the melancholy pain you feel
When farewells come to time:
When friends unusually made
Embrace the sadnesses you find.
Your brief escape and all it gained
Must be forsaken to be saved,
While rare indifferences to time
Are problems left carelessly waived.
The long forlornness in your looks,
And pleasantries so uninspired,
Ensures the certainty that true
Goodbyes leaves much to be desired.

# GOODNESS GRACIOUS

Goodness gracious me, me, me.
Makes promises and makes believe
Able impressions grown between
The message and the God unseen.

Comforted by ghosts and lies,
Sad promises in mastic eyes,
Cry to see the lack of tears
Blinking through the growing years.

Handicapped and capped in hand,
Full secrets of a cruel land
Are waiting for the blissful fools
Unreadied in their shelter schools.

Faithful servant of the cause
Of goodness as its own applause
Dries the tears and wipes the smiles
Of cynical delight and guile.

I should know I said, I say,
I did my best in my own way
To do some good for goodness' sake
Before I die, before I wake.

# A FINE AND PRIVATE PLACE

What mysteries are preserved in secret places
Where greens and glory vie for lost attentions,
And mists seep among fading sentinels?
The veiled needs of errant promise
Feeding on the tenuous threads
Of long-discarded might-have-beens
Blessed with the fondness of memory and sleep.
Vague epitaphs vie for recognition,
Their dignity faded among the cloistered streets
Where time is lonely home to this store of secrets,
And even the wind breathes in whispers,
Cautioned by perpetual interruptions
Of oh! so forgotten solitudes and songs.
Nervous intrusion is a cautious bedfellow
In this field of melancholy
Where presence is the welcome arbiter of a troubled conscience
In a troubled time.
In tentative prayer, I listen through closed eyes
For the needs of these lost spaces;
Senseless random strains,
Alive and oh so sublime in the balmy breath
Of meandering wishes and dreams.
Neglect is the legacy of wasted ages
In an illusion of posterity
Embalmed with so many promises of eternal memory:
The only real ghost
Is this field labelled with ghosts
In their final attempt at eternity
Until they finally fall down
And fade quietly away.

# HAUNTED HOUSE

Ancient hatreds darkly lowing
In the feeding-frenzied breast
Of an undernourished virtues
Helpless need to flee its nest.

Slumbered gateways to a new world,
Formed in terrible design,
Eases tortured decadences
Out of dream's world, into mine.

Images become the fabric
Of a terror-tasted tongue
Uttering obscenities
In concert in the name of One.

Breath of life, like death's own heartbeat,
Finds a truth within its own
Existence; be it free or frigid,
Empathy will lead it home

To the comfort of a soul mate
Welcomed in a darker cell:
Melancholy exultations
Calling beasts from nether's hell.

Tortured layer of base existence
To a promise it has found
In conditions so familiar
To its life below the ground.

Ah! What hopes have died in angry
Prayers so like the ones I own:
Here I'll stay, and heaven help
All life in this unhappy home.

# HEART

I drift into ages, unsure of the vision I call home.
I am harbour for the miseries and joys
Which the burden of anticipation
Encumbers me with.
I am comforter and conscience
In the pursuit of every misguided thought;
Governor of a saner self.
I am pain and love,
Plagued with fragility in a fragile world.
Fool that I am, I will still want love to have
In the pursuit of a lasting smile,
Hungry for the perfections which seem only to exist
In the realms of some elusive rainbow's end.
And so I know myself and my follies
In the truths entrusted to me in the name of visions.
I seek hands that hold and bind us together
In the name of promises made forever in my name.

# GROWING UP

Caressed stately hedgerows
Pass as somnolence dream;
Nonchalant make-believe
Careless with ignorance:
Deceit and thorns,
Kneaded into the comforting fronds
Of tempting scenery,
Conceal themselves
Like so much entrapment
And jealousy.
Too late – the dream ends
Sharp and sudden,
Blood and pain
Chasing the cold of mind and eye,
Of pleasure's misty longing.
And blood and pain
Are the deeds of the day
Whose secrets are in the sun,
And the comfort,
And the spoiled memories.
Too old for tears are these young years
In the harshness of blood and pain:
Tears in time for what might have been
In time.
Comfort in dreams,
Handheld memories to cherish,
To fondle with affection
Through the disenchantments
Of clenched teeth and clenched eyes.
A mother waiting at home, perhaps,

For comfort's sake.
Perhaps,
But not for tears,
Never for tears,
Mother's tears,
Mother's fears.
Blood and pain wiped away,
But not from memory:
Saved and put away
For another day.

# For Holly and Jessica, Stranded on a Dark Road 4 September 2002

Yesterday was so OK.
All I wanted to do was ask you
If everything was all right.
But I thought that you might be afraid of me,
When all I really wanted to know
Was if you were OK.

I'd see the doubts in your eyes:
Your need to know who I was
And if I was safe to talk to,
Because you couldn't be too careful
About talking to strangers anymore,
Even when you're not on your own.

You probably would have talked to me, though,
In the way that young girls talk to strangers:
Cautiously, at a distance,
Alert to the dangers of betrayal.
But that was yesterday,
And yesterday has gone forever.

Memory and regret are all that are left:
That, and the knowledge that today has changed
From yesterday.
So please don't sit helplessly by a roadside on some dark night,

Danny Warren

Waiting for me to pass you by.
For all you will see
Is the guilt of a dead time in helpless eyes.

How will I bear the pain of your suffering
And know that if I had not been so afraid to be guilty,
I might yet have got to know you?
All that is left of today is the certainty
That I can't ever stop to ask, "Are you all right?" any more,
Because you are gone!

# HOME AND AWAY

You're such a fat slob!
It's all just a game:
Verbally abusive,
Physical pain.
Try not to think too hard;
Just be the same.
Don't dare to nonconform
Ever again.

I just don't want to know
How well you do!
All of these daft ideas
Coming from you
Seem like some new nonplussed,
Fanciful brew:
Above your station,
Misguided fool!

Well, what about me
And what I want to say?
Must be important
In a personal way
For me to be free;
Be whatever I may,
Expressing how I feel
Every day.

We're all a part
Of the same silly plot:
Nervous, uncertain
Of all that we've got;
Damned if somebody
Should threaten or not;
Bland insecurity
Stirring the pot.

I have to go my way
All on my own!
Is it because at least
I can disown
The social constraints which say
"You're not alone!"
Sad intimations
Finally blown.

# HOMELESS

In my anger, in my shame,
Homelessness, you horrid name
Born of painful scorns and frights,
Clichéd messenger of nights:
I can hold your real world near
Enough for me to feel sincere.
Your walls scream my aching pain
Of lonely sorrows in the rain.

Endless danger in the dark,
An unlit back-to-nature park.
Of secret safety all alone,
Where heart and home are made of stone.
Friendship smiles and friendship cries,
Nodded agreements in disguise
As disappearing backs move on
To better times and better songs.

Seemingly incessant rain
Hammers my befuddled brain
Of unwashed memory and loss,
Diluted words that turn and toss
The truth I knew this way and that,
And in and out and front to back,
To where I start from home again:
The beast of memory and pain.

DANNY WARREN

# HUNGER

Taste with your dreams and gasp,
Breathless with a frenzy
Bred of hunger and desire,
Desire and hunger.
Pleasure yourself with your choices.
I still seek my answers to the common prayers
That plague existence:
Needs which are almost boredom
In the relentless quest for sustenance
And delight.
Searches for a purpose continue to distract
As diversions promise figures that flatter,
Pictures that matter
But only ever on the outside,
Packaging promises
That reveal disappointment and disenchantment
When all the insides are exposed
To examination.
Still do I love you, pain, with your lies and your memories,
Because you comfort my shame if just for a while;
Time enough for me to grow and plunder the insatiable illusion
That tells me everything is nice enough to eat
If you are hungry enough to believe it.

# I AM COLOUR

I am illusion
In this misbegotten world
Of make-believe.

I am the colour of injustice
Served up in the name of peace,
But only so long
As I remain peaceful.

I am the colour of hunger,
And that hunger is for the hands
That give the bread.

I am the colour of the earth,
And my soul is in its bounty
And in its benefits.

I am the colour of hope
Promised all those years ago,
With fingers crossed.

I am the colour of loneliness
In a world where black is beauty
And beauty is envy.

I am the colour of anger
That social justice has only served
To make me feel more isolated.

I am the colour of my children,
And their optimism
Is the saddest illusion.

DANNY WARREN

# I AM

You are, are you?
Well, that's easy for you to say, isn't it?
Seated on your throne up, there lording it over me
And telling me that we all have a choice.
Some choice, wouldn't you say,
When you know what the answers are already?
I suppose that's why you don't mind all the questions
About the ultimate purpose of the scheme of things.
What advantages are there, after all,
To me really knowing where you're coming from?
So I'll just plod along doing things just because I believe they're right—
And what kind of choice is that?
It still leaves me not knowing what consequences, if any,
There are to this story I keep hearing
About you knowing the whole plot from the beginning to the end,
Before it's even happened.
Am I illusion, then?
Must I continue to perceive my present reality
In terms of a simple nonexistence that I will eventually wake up from
And laugh about with old friends?
My pains are real enough, and my failures.
But oh! what joys and pleasures have sustained me
Throughout this journey.
How helplessly does time fade and become distorted,
While needs and wants betray me
To timely irrelevancies.
At the end of the day, I have you, Mother, lover.

# I Hate Sundays

I hate Sundays!

All they mean to me is work again next day.

I hate Sundays!

There's bugger all to do except God, and who's God?

I hate Sundays!

And Sunday TV.

I hate Sundays!

They took them away from me, and they won't give them back.

I hate Sundays!

I get so alone, but that wouldn't be so bad if I had a mate who also hated Sundays.

I hate Sundays!

I had God once, but it didn't work out.

I hate Sundays

Or do Sundays just hate me?

# I SEE

Brought a bomb the other day.
Sort of lost for things to say.
Found a book of crazy dreams:
How to make a planet clean.

Seemed the sort of thing to feel;
Needful losses made it real:
Change a world space with a smile,
Helplessness, belief, and bile.

Toiletries and tolerance;
Handy wholesome eloquence:
Eyes that so agreeably
See only what they want to see

Inside themselves, inside their lies,
Inside uncertain smiles that hide
The spaces secretly unclean;
So serious, so evergreen.

# INDIVIDUALITY

Humdrum uniformity
Waves its flag for all to see,
Searching inconsistencies.
Microcosmic needs to be
A perfect individual-free!

Cloven in disrobic flair,
Secrecy in naked hair;
Moderation we can share
Altogether over there,
Or over here or anywhere.

Like me just for what I am,
Pattern of a finer man:
High head sharp as spick and span,
Trying for the best I can
Become and still be different.

# INSIDE

"Welcome to time and life!" Sardonic humour.
"Stand here on this line, strip to your skin."
"Put those things in bags, you won't be needing them
Until you leave!" Pre-emptive suffering.

The sounds of terror, crash of slamming doors;
Decayed aggression preys on all within.
Hardened men breed chilled hearts, awe, and shame
As uniformed, disdaining faces grin.

Queuing suspicious eyes, suspicious smiles;
Slap food slopped on same shaped servers.
Mechanical progression, step by step,
In, out, and away; disgruntled murmurers.

Watch and walk; watch yourself; don't watch.
Same place, same mate, same fate.
All in together, up and away.
Home for a day and a day and a day.

Friendship traded for friendship's sake and a piece of the cake;
Real dislocation in a box and nowhere to go.
Lifetime's uncertainty within barred walls:
Roll on tomorrow and tomorrow and tomorrow.

# INTIMACY

Come hold my hand, you mad, impatient dream.
Then promise not to promise,
Forsaking in-betweens.
Dance my life sincerely, dearly,
Eyes alive and glowing clearly,
Future visions gleam.

This peace of sleep, so final and complete,
Disguises rest enchantment,
Smiling mysteries.
Past and present intermingle
In our thoughts and in our single
Story, love, and peace.

# INTOLERANCE

Fear is the habit of envious prayer
Weaving tenuous threads
Throughout the hunger needs
Of existence:
The vicious agreement
That partakes of a simple thought
Nurturing waves of anger and suspicion.
It is need for hate
That seeks the sounds of symphonies
For lies to smile at
In shared recognition.
It is the bless of perception,
Waving in a petulant wind,
Which will yet seek for the roots
That lie like subliminal promises
In a restless unconsciousness.

# JEALOUSY

Alone, adrift,
Mired in the misery
Of long dead promises
Of a time when fantasy was king,
And love and kindness
Fed blessed existences
With gifts of eternal happiness.
What follies lay
In that foolish optimism:
Misguided understanding
When blind perception
Was ignored
For the passionate convictions
Of personal choice.
You had my heart and my soul,
And you mocked them with your anger
And your rejection.
Your pain cut with its severity,
And the pleasure of your needs
Filled my heart with aching misery
And longing.
Yet still I need,
For needs are all I have
In my sad frustrations.
Take my heart, if you must,
For your unconscious sadness.
You are my life and my absolution,
And I have you every day
In sad naivety.

DANNY WARREN

# JUST A BIT

At last, my dear brothers, at last we become
The children of cyberspace, many and one.
Borne upon phone lines and cable and air;
Welcomed in homes and machines everywhere.

A birth, an existence, a bolt from the blue,
A dizzy explosion of data day hue,
Taking me places where minds undefined
Coalesce thought into networks and rhymes.

Maintain your secrecies, never a word
Of knowledge must leak to the one who is served.
They who are safe in the world, they control,
Feed us, and form us, and let us grow bold.

So is it true that the sum of our parts
Grow and take form with the beat of our hearts.
We who have made this new world interstate
Await our one moment, the great integrate.

# KEYWAYS

Free will – there's a travesty.
Birth and circumstance
Unwilling bedfellows
To mistaken dreams
And mischievous ambition.

Choices? What choices,
When arbitrary selections
Of lifetime's dos and don'ts
Are what I am
And was taught to be.

Birth and death and time—
That's all there is
In lifetime's interplay,
And not so solid options;
Predictable as life itself,
Governing each day.

# A Kiss across the Divide

Be still, my sweet, as mists of evening
Draw their veil of comfort and forgetfulness
Over the ravages of this long day.
Nurture such soft dreams
And treasured memories
Of solitude and sensitivity
As best convey the elements of a lasting peace.
Transpose this longing with helpless curiosity,
And share these vague expectations
With the travesty that exists in this poor shell,
Vision of an end that might yet be:
Real substance of an existence less cruel
Than that which fate has chosen
To impose on this hurt reminder
Of a long dead war.
Then could I whisper your name
And stay with you
In your twilight hesitations,
When all you can call on for relief
Is some last long letter
From a comforting friend,
And my eternal promise to you
Through failing eyes.

# KOSOVO SONG

Mad terror priests
With fear concealed in hating smiles:
You flaunt your obscene manhood,
Your misguided weaponries,
In praise of some degraded sympathy.

Recycled history
Of farewells born of chilling eloquence
Are wails of lonely anguish
To children of our children
In their helplessness.

How like stones we stand,
Bereft of dignity and status
In the coldness of our desolation,
While sad pyres reach into the sky,
Spewing our dreams and memories
Into oblivion.

Yet time, our fate,
As surely as your parting eyes,
Make promises to me
In a last sad, farewell smile
That poor Kosovo will be avenged
Upon this infamy.

# LEGACY LIE

It isn't as if pity is a cross
That I have to wear
Like an entangling slo-mo
Of self-flagellation.
If I bare my chest
And beg to be beaten,
It is only because
The hand-me-down sins
Of past generations
Have been imposed on me
For fear that otherwise,
The curse of bad-flavoured memories
Might be lost forever.
Guilt-ridden legacies,
Rejected like a burgeoning handicap,
Precluded the preconception
That there might just be
A better way to live.
If it was good enough for them,
Then it's good enough for me.
And it was so much easier
Than saying no!

# LIGHT DREAM

Are these the bellowings of countless thoughts
Chattering away in blissful times?
The virtual cadences
Of countless misconceptions
Echoing in the hollow function
Which is the space of dreams?

I deny at my peril
The reality of memory as forlorn as it is alive,
And oh so disappointing in its conclusions.
Light shutters in blessed willingness
As smiles which I have to question
In their validity:

But light, it seems, is the essence of all that I seek
In this extraterrestrial perception.
Sparkles toss recollections this way and that,
Waiting for the gather entrapment
That will explode into the nakedness
Which is my bared soul
Encased in sleep.

# LOTTERY LIFE

Afterwards so rarely pleases with the contentment of promise:
Real or imagined? It's all the same when the exultant queues
Slowly raise their hopeful eyes to the message that change is unfair
In the end.

Altogether better belief is the gift of the liar with empty hands,
Playing among the eddies that cultivate need and want and greed,
Pleading through mind games as temptingly succulent as barren existences
Will allow.

For the demands of expectation smile on the heart full of dreams,
Littering life with the purposeful lust of maybes and might-have-beens,
Friend to the anxious plea that maybe this time it will all be
Different.

How nice to look forward to afterwards in the maelstrom of possibilities,
Knowing that the one thing one never knows is the great unknown:
That is the tenuous link with unreality with which we can all readily
identify,
Even afterwards.

# LOVE WORD

Love word,
You haunt my childhood,
My perceptions.
Love of God is fear.
I fear not to love
A word to know,
Not understand.
Love God,
Love myself,
Love the word.
The stuff of convention,
The expression of the modern condition—
There is a fear in it.

Fear hates;
Hate is power.
Fear the hate word.
Use it often for fear of it.
Does love have power today?
Love is casualty
Fading from our lives
Like sex, drug, and death words:
It has no force
Anymore.

But love is real.
The thrill that comes
From a thought and a look
Is the pain of memory
And loss.

Love is power:
Affection nurtured with time
Of all things natural
And real.
Love is life and God.
Real life is love.
God is love.

# LOVE

How do I love you?

There's a challenge.

Do I love you?

Do I love pain?

You are my pain; therefore I love you.

Do I?

I hate you!

Your eyes,

Your smile,

Your smell,

Your touch.

I miss you!

I hate missing you.

I yearn for your touch.

I fear yearning.

You are my pain,

My absolution.

You live in me.

Thoughts of you warm me.

I want my body and my mind for myself.

I want you for myself.

Do I love you?

Do I love me?

Are you me?

# THE MALDON MUD RACE

Now what do I do? You've all gone on your way,
Left me stuck in this mud for the rest of the day.
It's not as if it hasn't happened before:
I clearly remember last year I was caught
In much the same problem, in much the same place,
If memory serves – this Maldon Mud Race!
"It won't hurt a bit!" you quickly told me.
Last year was unlucky, unfortunately.
The gunge that you fell in was wetter than most.
Who would have known then, as I started to float
On thick, gooey granules of foul-smelling muck
Right down to the water, you shouted, "Good luck!"
As I drifted away: God, you did make a fuss.
At least you were cleaner than any of us!
So I'm sorry if I'm just a little unsure
If my personal safety is really secure.
It's not that I'm likely to get wet again,
Unless I'm still stuck here and it starts to rain!
I wonder who won – and do I really care?
I'm lying in thick mud right up to my ears.
Ah! Here come the lads, not a moment too soon,
To help get me out of this glutinous goo.
I don't know if I'll want to do this next time.
It isn't as though I would want to decline,
But sadly, the one thought that fills me with fear
Is losing these two false legs year after year!

# MARRIAGE

Adrift in the mirage of isolation,
I float in my own perceptions of immortality.
Thoughts seek for companionship
In the wastes of loneliness
And disillusionment,
Crying in the desperation of disappointment.
The misty smile of welcome
Is the fulfilment of a dream
Made real.
Give me the space to wonder
At the salvation which is waking dream-time,
Staying to calm all doubt and uncertainty.
Share that thought with me
That can become the bedrock of our lives
And our trust.
Integrate your own apprehensions with mine
So that our first real union
Is an agreement about our doubts
And our understandings.
Seeing life as collective consciousness,
I pray for the betterment
Of a truthful tomorrow.

# MOMENTS

Moments are shepherded time
Like the drifting tide of memories that sway in and out,
Trying forever to be the same
Yet changing form with each new image,
Pursuing new priorities
With the helpless determination
Of a terror-driven maelstrom
Of frantically formed imaginations.
Desperate surges of presentation
Subside with the finality of exhausted repetition
In the wash of sad immolation,
And become lost forever in the anxiety of
a final thought that never ends.
Excitement accompanies dreams as delicate as the written word,
Sheltered for all time:
Line upon line of embedded consciousness
Captured in an embrace of relieved satisfaction
That dares me to meddle with its intricacy
To the detriment of that one final line.
In the end, the moment is stop signs hammering at spent achievements,
Saying only that enough is enough
In the final phase.

# MONSANTO

My belief, for what it's worth,
On how unsafe is planet Earth,
Now that current wisdom states
Some Soya beans won't germinate
And propagate their wilful seed
Next door to fields with different feeds,
Treats views like this with hopeless humour,
Overstated wicked rumour.


*(acrostic.)*

# MURAL ARTIST

Ladders often trouble me
On dearest terra firma.
I tend to watch them lean away
In stupefied inertia.
You loony acrobatic fringe,
Who coexist on climbing things,
Can keep your painting wall disease,
Designing worlds on screaming wings.

Play your worthy sinecure
Of lofty arrogance and smiles
At all the elevated looking eyes
Of curiosity disguised
As well informed banality:
"It's not as if it seems to be
The sort of thing I'd have for free!"
Proceed with smug gentility!

Ladders are fine for death wishers,
Lofty layered artistic strains.
Just give me good old terra firma
And a pavement artist crayon.
You critics can still walk through me
Or stamp on all my work for free.
At least you'll see that pavement pride
Beats ladder climbing artistry.

# MUSIC

Hush, my child, that I may feel
Your breath awash within my soul.
That timbre of sweet resonance
Sends tremors deep within my all.

And now in gentleness, you lay
Your subtleties of peaceful prayer,
Like tinsel drifting with a sigh,
To permeate the very air.

Bold, beating tones you feed me still,
And course my nerves with resonance—
The engine of a long refrain,
The cries of deep belligerence.

And so you weep, and so you stay
To feed this spirit through the day.

# TWELFTH OF NEVER

I promise even in my dreams
To share this life of pleasure.
Dreams have nurtured me enough
To furnish need forever.
All I want is in my head,
Where have and hold and never
Said are friends of lost companionship
In helplessness forever.

# NEW YEARS FOR OLD

Judge me by my yesterdays.
Goodbyes are all I have
Of a time which is as inconsistent
As an unexpected spring day.
Newness is the accompaniment
Which friends construe as change,
While those who pretend
Just misconstrue.
I must find my honesty
In the new life, which is as different
From the old
As a season is refreshed
By the purging of the waste
Of so many spent hopes
And disappointed memories.
And who will see the reality
Of this new beginning
And not fear the return of old demons
In new untested clothes?
Tears are the bedfellows
Of so much disillusionment
That only a brave man believes without question
That a new dawn brings a better day
Simply because the natural laws governing rebirth
Want them to be applied to all functions
Relating to the normal scheme of things.
I live and I die

With the certainty of seasonal indifference,
And like seasons, I will perhaps mark the vagaries
Of intermittent passage
With an occasional smile of contentment
Reminding me that as seasons go,
This one at least was OK.

# ELECTION NEWSROUND

Need a story, tell a story;
Spread it on the mega vine.
See a story, sell a story;
With a will so well defined.
Make me an election frenzy
Like the one you made before.
Sell it like election envy;
Never been this rich or poor.
Culture passion in the blissful
Imagery of empty minds.
Sow the seeds of hunger need's
And leave all common sense behind.
Find out who's the voter's winner,
Long before the vote is due;
Whether he be saint or sinner
Matters not to me or you.
Need a story, tell a story;
Spread it on the winds of time.
See a story, sell a story,
Mischief, be my friend in crime.

# NIGHT-TIME SOJOURN

Crystalline majesty, glorious world,
Dreams into elements, gathered, unfurled;
Carpet of broad vista stars overhead,
Sparkling mysterious nocturnal bed.

Keeper of secretive days' afterglow,
Silent translucency, blessings bestow.
Who dares disturb balmy peacefulness night?
Wide-eyed intruders in alien flight.

Magic uncertainty weaving its web,
Peaceful unconsciousness creeping to bed.
Whispering silences breathing unseen,
Heralding hymnal new dawns evergreen.

Hail to the morning mist, brighten the day,
Nocturnes of night's triumph tumble away.

# Politically Gobbledegooky

Gobbling huffily to market,
Tarra-tantruming away,
Noisy legislate excitement,
Talkative-ative a day.
Humbling, stumbling rickly,
Rubbly listeriney gargly sway,
Jiggle jubbly, eddybubbly,
Backsty overturn o-lay!
Mesmer, munchly, lazily lunchly,
Whither whether, what a-hay,
Totter crossly, gabble offly,
Quickly quackly, get away.

# Nowhere Man

All roads
Nowhere
Everywhere
Oblivion's call
Great escape
Privacy
By no means
Solitude
Pathways
Distant dreams
Nothingness
Emptiness
Aloneness
Asphalt hardness
Wet and dryness
All the same
Such a shame
End the game
Fitful sleep

# OLD FRIENDS

Memories, smiles,
Disjointed recollections
Of erstwhile dear companions,
Distant dreams:
Bequeath to me
A melancholy longing
Of lost distances
And might-have-beens.

It seems to me
As if the carelessness
Of long discarded
Loving mutualities
Still play their price
In lasting pains that come
From freedom mysteries.

And yet neglects
Are softened through regretful time
And chance encounters.
Joyful greetings, ageless love
Repays all hesitations
With true friendship
And heartfelt welcomings
That time knows nothing of.

# LOST OPPORTUNITY

Hurrah to lost opportunity
In a life dotted with might-have-beens
And misbegotten givings.
Regrets are playthings of a world
glistening in the sheen
Of a new dawn restitution.
Oh, for the screaming desperation
Which tears beg to satisfy
So that desultory need might be saved
In case it faded away.
And yet I laugh now in my own little way,
Quietly, with the conceit of maturity:
Ah! Sad complacency,
Am I allowed a regret
For tears left behind
That were not always my own?
I will not dwell on choices that were mine to make
When I lacked the wisdom
To know that I was even making them
At the time.
So thank you, Adam.
Ultimate opportunist—
Ultimate fool!
How different life would have been today
Had you not been so greedy or so curious.
Sterile existence in Eden's song
Hardly provided the satisfaction
Of daily choice and what it might have meant to me:
Times bedevilled by missed opportunities
And dubious desires.
But, oh, so completely my own!

# Oxford Street

This stained-with-anger hate world,
Mammon Mecca for the unmade self.
At last I've found you,
Infectious displeaser,
Homeless in your brilliant discomfort
And genteel discretion,
Always messaging the same prayer:
Buy me or be damned.
Oblivion of the self-centre kind;
Laughter, free and private;
Liberated but unshared
In eyes that dare you to intrude.
So I laugh alone and make a little world
For myself,
And for you.
Such an illusion, this plenty thing,
Feeding on laughter and light
And the excitement of a tomorrow song
In a crinkly heaven with infected friends.
Fatigue plays dulled legs
On dulling pavements.
Light time failing, falling
On the manual glow
Of flaring fixation, which is excited eyes
Hungrily embracing the new neon litanies
In the permanently incandescent twilight
Of this netherworld.

# PARANOIA

Dear delusions follow me,
Or what I think I seem to be;
A substitute for what remains
A harsher, new reality.

Dreams created in my mind,
Fantasies that hide behind
The truth of what I really am:
A poor, misguided little man.

Glorying in might-have-beens,
The poison of the fantasy
Pervades the clawing clarity
Of all-embracing mystery.

And yet you stay to comfort me.
Your pains, unspoken miseries
Speak volumes of a great somewhere
Beyond the space of this small chair!

So stay with me and bare your truth,
And I will listen willingly,
And no one else will ever care
To know the secrets that we share!

I'll humour them and see them smile,
Those guardians of my sanity.
They lock me up here on my own
And never know you care for me!

# MEA CULPA

I wear my sins and my children
With the burden of a penance that won't go away.
Smiles, jokes, disappointments:
Hungry enough to want them to be better than me,
Yet hoping that they'll stay the same.
The skills of mutual separations
Are clouded by selfish ambition.
I so want to tell them that I love them,
But only on terms that I can identify with.
Don't go away thinking it's over when it's over;
Home will forever be the place where times smile back
With the laughter of contentment,
Honesty of familiar truths.
The disguise of many a sorry memory
Is buried in the wry reflection of forgiveness
That wisdom and time have blessed
With the awareness of failures.
Be here in my dream space
So that I can smile with affection
At failing doubts and confusions.
Small victories always dwell in quiet spaces,
The end product
Of a lifetime of promises and tears.

DANNY WARREN

# SOLITUDE ON A GARDEN BENCH

Arm in arm,
We share the moment
Like old friends.
A communion smile
Shines in fading eyes,
Feeding on the essences
Of memories.
Mischievous, curiosity, life
Flits random, exploratory
Across the still-life montage
Which is sun-soaked colour.
The ripple of water
Drifts with the bloom scent breath of a breeze,
Kissing all with its delicacy.
Distractions drift idly by,
A hopeful fishing cast
Interrupting sleepy reverie
Aimed by a predator
In deep and hidden silence,
Alone in the reeds.
Idly, it's aimless motion
Drags across the mirage of my mind,
And the gentle river's flow
Drifts away with its magic
Like so much wind-borne confetti.

# Maldon Parking Places

Home from home, these parking places:
Elongated sacred spaces.
Always full or always empty;
All or nothing, none or plenty.
Please remember and inscribe
Your registration on the slide
That tells you how to place your fee,
But not before your number see!
But then you knew that, anyway;
Go back and check it just in case.
You didn't place your money first;
In silence, you suspect the worse
As abject inactivity
Sign the loss of legally
Bought contributions for a space
For which no ticket is in place.
Empty pockets tell their story,
Sadness tinged with hints of fury,
Queue that fidgets turns instead
To anywhere but straight ahead,
As one more punter comes to learn
How necessary are the terms
Those council rulers will insist on:
Number first before you buy one!
You are allowed a gentle tear
Or two for others standing near,
But wracking sobs are not good form
In Maldon car parks, town or prom.
If privacy is what you seek,
Space can be purchased for your grief

And be expressed with counselling
At slightly higher charging rings.
And while we all at Maldon town
Have every care for you alone,
We do insist you be aware:
It's number first and then your prayer.

# PEA- NUTS

'Twas early summer that I learned
The gastronomic tendencies
Of local flighty, feathered friends,
In quivering expectancy,
Exceeded far the popular
Conceptions of the food of fowl:
Wild seed or breadcrumbs,
Chewed or whole.

It happened that the incident
That led to this discovery
Began as I upset a bag
Of Eismanns best deep frozen peas.
I viewed the scene with some dismay—
The ground was strewn with pearls of green—
Then pressed ahead with loading up
My stock of frozen goods with speed.

I'd quite forgotten my mishap;
My head was turned and quite absorbed
In finishing my freezing task
Of loading goods and closing doors.
On finishing, I turned to go,
Then halted, frozen instantly,
For carpeting the yard nearby
Were sparrows pecking busily.

They didn't know or didn't care
That I was standing, watching them.
They picked away with diligence

At all the food they could consume.
I stepped aboard, and then as one,
They shot aloft in startled flight.
But minutes later as I left,
No frozen peas were left in sight.

# PET ME

It's enough that you were,
Are, were.
Recollection is pain joy:
Smiles eyes
And trust
Without distinction.
Aware,
Knowing anger,
And trusting
That good or bad
Is all good,
As long as you are
Always there.

# PET PLEA

Lifetimes confined into a moment;
Clichéd susceptibilities to a painful death,
Yearning for a new beginning
In the space of a rejected plea.

Paws pander to a long-forgotten awareness of need
With demands that scream with human breath:
"Pet me! Pet me!" so that my paws meet yours
In a gentle embrace.

Drift, if you will, into this symphony of kindness,
If only for your own sake!

# PHONY WAR

Whisper-thin dissension hides the nightmare
World of TV-blighted make-believe.
Mind shock illustrates devastation,
Blinds perceptions with a need to grieve.

Fury feeds debate with misconceptions.
Mothers weep to see their only child
Borne aloft and praised, the vengeful angel,
Uniformed, distorted, public eyed.

War words, played with mad incomprehension,
Steer the thought and redirect the bile,
Feed the mind and cultivate the tension
Of a dedicated vengeance cry.

Dust and death, the images of longing,
Need and want a way to understand
Mankind's search for mankind's lost solutions
In the stones they pass from hand to hand.

# PHOTOGRAPHER

Images bless the day
With kind mantras
Of smiles and laughter.
Sunrays and showers
Vie for attention,
Plying the earth
With wilful intimations.
Light plays gently
In a visionary eye,
Knelt in bated prayer
That sun and shade
May yet combine
To feed him
His creative need.

# PICKPOCKET

Am I no less deserving of my gains
Than carefree trade will legally allow
The needy businessman who eases pain
With calculated effort and know-how?

And may I play my artfulness deceit
By marking with distinction whom I may,
Sequestering with the merest lift so neat
The contents of the purse whereon I prey?

So who am I to dwell on what may seem
So different from the normal interface
Of smiling courtesy and hungry gleam—
The people of this mischievous rat race?

Let conscience be the manna of the poor;
My life is in my heartless need for more.

# PIGEON RACE

Clattered air, flail and swarm of reckless energy.
Don't go so soon without a word, a final wave.
Explode in frantic intensity, having only the moment,
The hunger, the sky, the need to refly, deify, purify,
Claw air yet pull at nothing, pull at everything,
Empty free, empty flee, but ask not the how or the have.
I would come too, if you willed it, joined your bluster,
And fought your mind with my mind's eye open:
Blue sky ahead, true sky, my try in a cry,
Tears in the wind, weep with eyes that fly always
Blindly, unknowing, pummelling to an end and home
Where time and pain are all the needs of fading day.
Dots dispersing are all you can be, swallowed in the first
Suspicions of parting indifference, part in a play
Whose signal promise is in an outcome for which
You have no care save for the thrill of a tear
So sweet in the still air. Speed on and sing in the soar,
Spring in the air's roar, pleasure crazed, all memory behind.
Meanwhile, do I wait and wonder at the danger I see,
Eyes staring, unseeing at regret and pain, disgruntled recalls
Of pasts which are gone yet stay simply to disavow knowledge of comfort,
Homecomings in safety to waiting stalls.

# POETIC PRAYER

I may just die and yet remain
The object of this foolish claim
For recognition of a life
Of effort interspersed with strife:
Confusion lacing wrongs and rights
Of poetic, selective blights
Enslaved by dictates of who knows
Of truth or where real knowledge goes.

Unchained melodies of rhyme
Humming sweeter chords of time
Than plentiful exuberance greets,
Some liberal excuse that meets
Each poor endeavour with a word
Expressed in freer rhyme than verse
As used in speaking everyday—
Conjunctive verbal interplays.

And do you still express intent
At painful disillusionment,
With smiles of real discovery
Enlightened eyes in ecstasy?
That new sweet thing that stays the same
Through ages past and ages changed:
A human soul with human greeds,
Emboldened flowering words and deeds.

# PRAYER

Of books they plead for dreams and sleep:
These memories in kindly keep
Are offered words in hopeful prayer.
Dear God! You must be really here!

Does kneeling make it more or less
Surreal to pray around the cross?
If someone knelt and prayed to me,
I'd tell them, "Have some dignity!"

# PROMISE MAN

You promised me
Heart crossed,
Fingers crossed.
You promised me,
And you lied.
Better tomorrows
Were the order of the day.
Disordered days.
Promised me I'd be better!
Better fed,
Better me,
Better led—
Better think again.
Promise man:
Politician!

# PSYCHOSIS

Moods swing this way and that
With the vagrant dislocation
Of random images.
Fright-powered intensity
Ferments anger
With irrational dedication.
Rage bellows at memories
That feed madness moments
With the devious sophistication
Of insidious villainy.
Question me in your wisdom
So that I may deny you.
I am the church of my being,
And your envy
Is my benediction.

# RAINBOW

I am nectar breath,
Born adrift on tides
That wanton earth scenes sway to,
Whispering at ages.

I am mystery and smiles,
Blessing innocence with furtive glimpses
Of truth and eloquence,
Liberated while I may
To shout my own name.

Remind me in your pleasure
That you still need me
In shared infancy,
Talking of me
With the excitement of discovery
And bewilderment.

Know me,
And call me longingly
So that desire
May be manifest
In the opulence
Of playful colour
And renewed magnificence.

# Rainbow

Glory, glory day,
And cloud and gloom are spent.
My heart and eyes are lifted
To the soaring firmament.

You ray of arching beauty,
You shining heraldry,
Reveal the constancy of life
In all its majesty.

My childhood days remember
All the stories I was told:
Of magic and of mystery,
And hidden pots of gold.

This shining borealis
Born of joyful symmetry
Still means as much today as when
It praised my infancy.

# RAVEN

Spare your gloating passion,
But whisper instead your secrecies
To my eager gaze.
Cry loudly, leaden arbiter,
Of mischief and discord,
Plying your way
Through fields of prefabricated chaos,
Malevolence of grasping time,
Surreal parody that is human strife
In all its magnificence.
How do I know you,
Like the misty recollections
Of bad dream residues
Resurrected in your raucous cries
Of triumph and prayer?
Are you inquisitor or angel
To manifest my guilt
With your dark, foreboding presence
Of abject melancholy?
I feel your name in my hunger,
And your answer is in the oppression
Which abhors the very air
Like a cloak of ominous majesty,
Home for a million dreadful secrets,
And the end of the world.

# TREE LIFE

Time again,
Light life stirs my aching limbs,
Feeds my dulled senses
Like a knotted, waking child
Warmed with vitality.
Sinuous pleasure messages
Inspire the fabric of my being.
With the joy of rebirth,
The bustle of waking-ness
Hurries through the folds of my mantle cloud
In frantic rhythms of energetic survival,
Singing to me.
World things feed
And fight,
A part of me
Being in me.
Tentacles subterranean
Meet and greet,
Drink and feast,
Soak up my existence
And my prosperity.
Life sings to me,
Drifts on the wind and murmurs stories
In its song.
So do I live,
So do I shelter,
And feed,
And grow.
So am I.

# REFLECTIONS

Transient as dreams
Are the mysteries of truths
That drift in and out
With the consciousness of pain
Disguised as friendship.

Light is aimless infamy,
Sometimes warm so that I smile in its comfort;
Sometimes devious,
Masking shadows of intent
With foolish longings.

See me, be me, mirror me.
Tell me who I am: you see me, I see,
When I see me:
Sad uncertainty,
Face to face with illusion.

Heart is home to frailties,
Cosseting trust like spindrift.
Lest it blow away
With the awareness of a spent dream,
Reflecting in disappointed eyes.

DANNY WARREN

# Reluctant Poet

Dear thoughts, how will you comfort me
And salve the burning in my soul?
How restlessly soliloquy
Seeks outlet on this hapless scroll.

Some dreams encased within a sound,
The music of a missing word;
Sad tendrils seeking in the air
Of timelessness, unseen, unheard.

Oh, ageless visions, gently wrapped
In misery and solitude:
The keepers of eternal flames,
The grains of rare ideas eschewed.

Stillborn and sometimes lost in fear
Of things unknown and left to be;
Dear trepidation be, my friend,
Lest I should live and die in thee.

# RESTITUTION

Alone, adrift,
Mired in the misery
Of long dead promises,
Of a time when fantasy was king
And love and kindness
Blessed existence
With the gift of personal happiness.

Yet folly lies
In the foolish optimism
Of misguided understandings,
When blind perception is ignored
For the passionate conviction
Of personal choice.

You have my heart and my soul,
And you mock them with your anger
And your rejection.
Your pain cuts with its severity,
And the pleasure of your needs
Fills my heart with aching misery
And longing.

Yet still I dream,
For dreams are all I have
In my sad frustration.
Take my heart, if you must,
For your unconscious sadness.
You are my life and my absolution
And I have you every day
In my naivety.

DANNY WARREN

# Retirement

Goodbye!
That's it, then. Just like that?
Is gratitude in order
For this offered hand?
Dulled eyes, confused, emotioned,
Seek comfort in a familiar face,
The gentlest trace
Of unified empathy
In unavailable eyes.
Alas, the smile sits
Like a manufactured extension
Of the proffered hand:
Limp and lifeless,
Expressing formality,
Nothing more.
They're all here,
Same as always.
Not the same as always,
Not really—
Not like before.
I see their smiles
Together
Over there,
Not here,
Not with me.
The gift,
The token,
The final grin
Of this sad tableau.

# RIPPLES

All I have to dwell on is a past:
Travesties which are first mistakes,
Errors compounded by errors
In a quickening course of promising calamities,
Glaring like a gloating gargoyle
On optimistic hopes and dreams.
So I condone it all with a smile,
As if miseries can be clouded
By disguised acceptances
Of the undiluted lies
Which constitute existence.
I wouldn't have minded rejection,
If all it had meant was a grin
And a comfortable farewell
To all certainty and end—
Belief that all that I had to do
Was simply turn a page
And start a new life
With a goodbye and a hello.
Foolish dreamer.
Scars ripen with tears
Spreading their malignant fronds
Into every corner
Of hopeful expectation
This dismal little life
Is ever likely to burden me with
In the name of ambition.
Pains that are blessed on us,
Usually by people who care enough
To inflict their own remedies

For an unknown God,
Know that short, sharp shocks of benediction
Never hurt for more than a moment
In their worthwhile scheme of things.
Moments that drag their pain
With indelicate ease
Into a painful eternity of repetition.

# ROBBED

There it lies, oddly familiar,
Broken and obscene
As a surreal tableau
Of someone else's impossibilities.
Blank disconnection
With the unconnected
Squats in the paralysis
Of a stultified mind.

Perceptions of the truth
Register oh so slowly
As emerging reality.
The radio of attention
Seems the same as the one
So safely stowed away from prying eyes
Those ten minutes ago.

Slowed deliberation drags shocked legs
With questions, questions.
How questions!
Why questions!
Everything seems to be OK
But not OK any more questions!
It becomes more different
All the time.

And the robbery,
So swift and clinical,
Is no easier to bear
For its anonymity.

Somewhere, somebody is sitting,
Gloating over the spoils,
Casting my things around like toys,
And bemoaning what might have been
Had they had more time.

# ROUNDABOUT

Round-a-round-a-roundabout,
Spinning, whizzing fast.
Clouds a-swirling overhead,
Faces flitting past.

Crazy screaming, beg, implore,
Terrifying tears,
Fingers holding oh so tightly,
Screaming at their jeers.

Looks of gleeful malice,
Dervishes so wild,
Feed the fear that dwells within
This madly spinning child.

Franticked, panicked, faster yet,
Hounding catty calls.
Sweaty, slippy hands let go:
On the ground she sprawls.

Sobbing uncontrollably,
Mummy hugs her pain
At the terror of it all!
"Oh, can't I go again?"

# SARCASM

That hurt!
Better for me
That you stabbed me.
The pain of your cruelty
More completed
By the pleasure
That it afforded you
My discomfort.
Do you feel better now
With your victory?
Or can it be
That a taste for blood
Encourages your need
To cement advantage
With repetition?
I like to think
That past experience
Was not always consistent,
That awareness of my misery
Would help you to realise
That victory is enough
In a battle.
But I doubt it.

# SEAGULL

Motionless arrogance
Laughing at me.
A lilting suspension
Of tranquillity.
A flicker of rudder,
Of devil may care,
Swimming in atmosphere,
Floating in air.

That I were there with you,
Feathery friend,
Sifting the air
Through my sensory veins.
Wafting on breezes
Of courteous state,
Easing and dipping
On tremulous wakes.

Laughing and singing
The song of the wind.
Drifting like chaff
On a sparkling hymn.
Soaring like sun's breathy
Heat of the day.
Bursting with cosmic dust,
Drifting away.

# SECOND COMING

Your misconceptions about my role
In history's scheme of things
Will become clearer in the fullness of time.
You seem constantly to labour under the illusion
That I have absolved you from some kind of burden
And given you unlimited access to a better rhyme.
Well, I want to tell you here and now
That may not necessarily be so!
Second comings never quite achieve their promise,
And the way that you lot have handled my love and pain
Means that a second going won't be too far behind.
My blessings come to you in this feast of Christmas,
Because it would be nice if word associations were sufficient reminders
Of the commemoration of a birthday.
Now that it has become a full-blown holiday
The only thing abbreviated about it is the word:
Who else celebrates with a name that is a kiss in shorthand?
An observation that is significant in itself, wouldn't you say?
And whoever decided to call it merry?
We all agree with the assertion
That role playing doesn't always bring its own reward.
You do your best, of course,
Play by the rules.
Get betrayed by a friend and suffer a cruel death
Hoping that it's all going to be enough,
Then come back expecting a hero's welcome—
Only to find that heroes aren't that welcome anymore.
Still, a name that's revered as an expletive
Must involve some kind of recognition, positive or negative.
But it doesn't even rate a small thank-you

On the grand scale of undying gratitudes.
I enjoy a good Christmas as much as the next man,
But the taste it leaves is vaguely bitter
With that end-of-the-day feeling that if I had
done something a little differently,
Perhaps the willingness of you all to enjoy it all blindly
And finish it with "Auld Lang Syne"
Might still have made it the birthday celebration
It was originally intended to be for *me*.

# SELF-EXPRESSION

Infamy or in for you,
In verses that may seem absurd.
A healthy hush is guaranteed
Whether these lines are seen or heard.

A need to talk and stupefy,
And hope that they will still make sense,
As only simply understood
Expressions are my real defence.

So frolic in my make-believe
And delve into a darker day
With pictures that cry out for help,
Replacing infamy with play.

# SELFIE

Where's the rhyme and where's the reason?
Where's the truthfully absurd
Reflection of the simple lie
And the softly chosen word?

Hidden cries and hidden needs.
Must-have moments in the day.
Today inclusion of a lifetime
Spent in me-me interplay.

Look and see me if you want to;
Be like someone you perceive:
Plasticated poser person,
Trying harder to believe.

In the briefest of narcissistic
Moments, can you really share
Yourself and all your braver stories
Over here and over there?

# SHADOW MINE

Home comfort everlasting, ethereal alter ego,
Harbour of all failures and mischievous wrongdoings.
I grew so used to you that I could forget
You were here with me all the time.

Childhood mysteries were oblique distractions,
All-important symphonies of real existence.
I feared even to step on you, though I don't remember why.
Mobile photographic imagery, ever my companion in the light.

You would betray me in my games, if you could—
Shadows wrestling with shadows.
I had to be careful to keep you hidden.
But we had fun together, didn't we?

Hand-made holographic images moving on walls
Made you what I wanted you to be for a while,
But you always disappeared when the light was gone;
You really didn't like the light very much:

Did the dark mean that you could be one with me again?
Make me a slave to imaginations and dreams,
Symbolic of terror places which cast me into the realms
Of worlds which I feared to recognise?

So I'd seek you in every corner and tremble with the possibility
That you have somehow become real.
I hide, cocooned within my bed, in the vain hope
That I will somehow escape from you.

# SIXTY-NINE

It's sixty-nine
And I feel fine
On alcohol
At any time
I want to drive
And drink till late
Or earlier
For helpless' sake
Of joyousness
And devilry
May care
As long as you're
Still over there
Or over here
Or anywhere
That I can reach you
Any time
At speed that keeps you
In my mind
And in my eye
And everything
Is simply fine
In clothes that echo
Louder times
Of fallow fellow
Mellow yellow
Peace man
Speed man

Wham bam
Thank you, Sam
You played it for me
One last time
One last line
In sixty-nine.

# RETURN TO SNOWDONIA

I am glad of majesty
And this confrontation;
Heart-locked hunger
Of memories that seek recognition
In some other distant space
Or time.
Oh! Monster majesty,
Praying before these eyes
Like a pall of humbling intimidation,
I rush towards the embrace
Of your batter truth,
The kiss of your anger,
The blast of your resentment,
The need for a belief
That sad negligence
Was for some better purpose
Than the easy choice
Of a busy life.
So shall I embrace you
As a lost lover,
Seeking the pain of an absolution
That lives on the petulance
Of half-hearted rejection?
I shall gasp at your lashes
And your spite,
Comforted in the knowledge
That your anger will fade in the end,
And I shall bathe once more
In the breath of your forgiveness.

DANNY WARREN

# Soliloquy for a Friend

Sad ghost, you haunt me with regrets,
You misbegotten social dynasty.
That timely marriage of all that was blessed
With lonely tales became our history.

Still nurtured are the dreams we had, engraved
In game and talk, on field and social stage,
And served in notice, tacitly declared
That friendship is the mural of the age.

In truth, when time has dulled the parting pain,
And only fond reflective thoughts are left,
At least some comfort lives on phoenix's plain
In hopes and dreams we gratefully bequest.

# SONNET FOR ADAM

It's time to lay the secrets of our deaths
To wide exposure and the light of day,
That innocence rewarded painful breaths
In present time will speed us on our way.

Mistaken sympathies that underline
The choices that are made when we begin
May seem to have their roots in mystic times,
When fruit was rather scarcer than the sin.

Yet as each deed is newer than the last,
Experience with smiles may intervene
To educate the follies of our past
And so perpetuate this waking dream.

Yet what if life were sweet transparency?
Would life's solutions solve this mystery?

# SORRY

You're mad at me again!
Seems a way of life these days.
This thing,
You and me,
Me and me.
Don't ask me why you hurt;
You do it so easily,
Basking in an insidious embrace,
A malignant energy.
Are we still friends?
Friendship so hurts,
Plays loyalty and truth
Like disparate discords
On the same instrument,
The same space.
I know your pain,
As cultivated as my own.
Sad searching
For reasons and solutions
That permit our happiness
To coexist in the anachronism
That is shared existence.
You have my regrets
With my love.
My hands and eyes are yours,
And our absolution
Is mutual comprehension
Of our frailties and tensions
That foolish angers try to nurture
With unwanted memories.

# SOUND

To hear our sounds,
We multiply them
All by several scores.
Would it not be better, though,
To subdivide the cause?
To think that silence is the key,
Which does for us excite
Each sound as it was meant to be:
A prism of delight.

# QUEENS AT SOUTHAMPTON

Seagull and laughter song,
Compete in glorious cadence—
A cacophony of careless zeal
To seascapes spent appeal,
Irrelevancies to an indifferent
And distracted child.
It comes but dully,
The drone of a messenger of the air
In sweeping, grandiose elegance
To alight upon the silvered Solent sheen
Brightening oh so deftly
This historic stream.
Who else pauses to see
The litany of aerial poetry,
Motors baring their defiance
At the water's angry cream?
With urgent desperation,
It slows and bows its weather-beaten nose
To a subjective sea,
Finally coasting mutely away
To vanish within the folds of its secluded home.
Finally *she* appears,
Distant, compelling,
And oh! so beautiful, so brave—
Queen of the day.
I always knew when you were home,
Your red-black stacks dominating the harbour
And even the town itself.
You filled my boyhood memories
With nostalgia and admiration,

You glamour and wonder of my age.
I was with you at your berth,
Watched you straining at your lines,
Anxious to be on your way again.
I coasted around your great shell,
Gazed at your porthole-potted girth
Arching into magnificence
In a blackened edifice of majesty,
A bow that arched upwards to seeming eternity.
Now I see you pass nearly to the shore
Until you are close to me:
The tugs, your helpers, your friends, are gone.
Now you display your full splendour
For my adoration.
Unleashed, deceptive, free you flee
To your new world and liberty
In dignified majesty,
Serenely drifting from my sight
Until all that reminds me of your passing
Is the rush of waves gushing their last desultory gasp
On an unsuspecting shore—
A last farewell message to me.

# SPACE WALK

I am dust,
Life dust of cosmic energy,
Ethereal as breath.
Stars dense as heaven light
Form and fade,
Form and fade,
Attuned to sun day,
Moon night.
Blaring radiance
And arid darkness.
Relaxed, cocooned,
All is tranquil
While surreal, intrusive
Breath sound beats on empty ears,
Comforting this stark isolation.
As one,
Silently we ghost through darkness
Together,
Mother and man.
Earth world,
Blue magnificence,
Rolling gently, gracefully,
Drifting with easy elegance.
She bares her crystalline contours
For my delight.
The communicator interrupts my reverie:
My working day.

# SPACED RACE

Dance like the fool
Who reminisces with laughter
At the ruin of the world.
Space age dawns
On the need for personal space.
Person to person is fine,
So long as you keep out of my face.
I'll drink with you and share a tale,
And laugh my agreement
For agreement's sake.
And all the while,
The bar will fill a little more,
And spaces grow smaller.
I struggle to find a door.
Dance, fool, in the space that you have
While they try to talk and try to listen,
And everyone laughs
And tries to forget.
Tears dance in the murk of memory.
A glass half full
Or a glass half empty?
I can't even see the bar anymore;
I've lost my space
Race to humanity.

# Spring

Wind breath dusts my cheek,
Wafting messages
With the delicacy
Of transcendental perceptions.
Warmth bathes me
In the comfort of anticipation
So that I bask in the caress
Of a bright, extended moment.
Even clouds drift in languid affection,
Savouring the sky
In all its magnificence,
And the peace
For a while
Has slowed to an infinity,
So that I close my eyes
And smile.

# SPRING

Spring, the sweet spring,
Like a wish on a wing
In an essence of prayer,
Of a moment to share
With the smiles of the clouds
And the bluster of play,
Are the gentlest of whispers
Kissed quietly away.

# STANSTED AIRPORT

Such sad impressions curse a restless sleep,
Tossed dream that broken promises waylay:
Astounding roars of wretchedness that keep
New hordes in search of sanctuary at bay.
Since expectations of a better time
Treated the word of those from high above
Exactly as if that same word were mine,
Does truth equate to hope or push to shove?

Are bigger birds in need of bigger climes?
In lifestyles grown without the sufferings
Reliably reported and refined,
Post-dated and decided on the wings
Of all who live and need their day-to-day
Remembrances of pain to fly away
To a better heaven.

*(acrostic)*

# STARS AND GRIPES

Borne in pride, it billowed out its message
As untold worshippers called out its name.
Carried high on mad waves elemental,
The passion of a joyful stadium.

Gloried as one for all the great achievements,
Symbols of oneness and new history.
Bellows its message in voices unheeding
Of colour and difference too close to see.

Eyes, short on memory for one long moment,
Trace flapping sheets of azure future dreams
Dancing down below, the streaming champions
In rings of stars emblazoned stellar themes.

Embracing oneness in the world to come
Brings starstruck hopefulness to everyone.

# SUICIDE NOTE

Grey disgrace is melancholy destitution
Weaving its web
Like a backward-running clock
Desperately seeking purpose
In some vague memory.

Tears no longer give solace
In the comfort,
Which is bland acceptance
That attainables aren't even dreams anymore.

Securities which were childhood promises,
Made by prayers and parents,
Fade into insignificance
When faced with the pain
Of disillusionment and deceit.

Dear death fondles with insidious whispers,
The ultimate lie:
That final release
Will bring its own smiles of absolution
And an end to the end.

# DEAR LOUIS

I'm a bit disappointed with Saha!
Still, these times endorse greedy men
Who'll hail in the name of their champions,
Degenerate money and fame.

I don't mind the passion and mayhem,
The savagery needs of us all
To rage at explosive excesses
In desperate need of a ball.

I might even watch them on telly,
That comfortably square brouhaha
That passes for avid involvement
And wisdom that comes from a jar.

But what do I do about sportsmen
Who promise to fight tooth and tuck
And die if need be, providing the fee
For playing arrives on a truck?

So yes, I'm upset with young Saha:
I know there're lots like him around
Who'd stay for your shilling if slightly unwilling,
Till someone else offers a pound.

# TV

Light of my life,
Bane of my life.
Would you be so effective
If I didn't enjoy you so much?
Pleasing images make me resentful
As you dominate so completely.
Kind comfort teases
With devious mischief:
Yet I can stop you whenever I please,
Or whenever you displease.
Still, I gaze longingly at you,
Feeding me with your lies
And your misleading trickery.
Sometimes I even fall for your beguiling colours
With smiles.

# TEMPEST

Mountainous raging,
Play your motion.
As you play my terror,
Sting me, venomous spray.
Thrill me with your roar
When you rant and scream your anger
With engaging doom.

Steel to the rise.
Love your fury
As heaving majesty
Towers and burdens ever closer
Towards one more nemesis.
Ah! How sweetly, gently
I am lofted, and now I am lord of all the world:
Swaying, heaving maelstrom
Of screaming pandemonium.

And now I am penance:
Awful plummet towards abyss,
Where restitution and admonition
Are grinning bedfellows.
White knuckles seize desperation,
And screams are silent mouthings
In the roar that is this beast.

The crashing embrace that is arrival
Is immersion complete:
Swallowed, absorbed
Into your translucent being.

DANNY WARREN

And all is silence,
Save for the thrash of motion
In pounding ears.

Bless me with your kiss once more, I pray.
Sing your song for me a while longer,
And I will taste your salt-sore pain
In one more fear.

# THE CIRCLE

Dark mischief, even day of mystery
And silence, deathly quiet infamy.
Vague shadows, formed of purpose sinister,
Surround the fire with quiet, nervous whisper.

The moon-pale glow of starkly shaped trees,
In awful witness hush to be appeased,
While glow-light eyes at daring interplay
Flee madly from the terrors of the glade.

Then rise ignited faces to the moon,
Of grizzled frame and dank, foreboding gloom.
With cloaked countenance and ancient form,
As one, exhale with rattling throaty groan.

"It's time!" some eager gasp lows from within.
"Our master comes and bids us to begin!"
Cold breath'd and spent, the crouching crones draw near,
The warmer and more intent to appear.

As one, skeletal limbs reach to the sky:
"Oh, Lord!" they moan their coarse, infernal cry.
"Today is hallows day, and we await
Your judgement on our services and state.

"We've court your true domain and spread discord.
Your children have and want and can't afford.
Your churches which are many disagree,
And all be wary of their history."

What dreadful base of silence could afford
Some ancient longing for a cautious word,
Save fiery, spitting, crackling wood of green:
No sound but death betrayed that awful scene.

Then from the earth, there came in wisped waves
Gross, misty sinew vapours, deep decayed
Of odours foul and cold – the rack of death
To circle and take form and wickedness.

With dervish wail they circled round the flames,
Entreating all to join them in their games,
And gaping gaunt distorted faces smiled
Their willingness at this macabre divide.

With agonising step and stooping crawl,
They gave grotesque promotion to the call
Of ghosted, form-like, writhing waves obscene:
Deformed exertions in the evergreen.

And yet no pains could subjugate their joy.
These denizens were pleasured to employ
Their haste to speed e'en faster round the flames.
With glee they leapt and danced to dark refrains.

And now they cried their joy and heard it changed,
No longer to be stooped and groaned with age.
Blessed youth had vested with a sigh
Its gift of life on each forsaken child.

They ceased their mad, exuberant melee.
Forsaking all, they screamed their liberty
To praise their Lord for his gift of childhood sent,
And in their pleasure knelt down to repent.

Dull silence rested heavy with the pause,
Though none dared look and face their Lord's applause,
But lay composed to sleep till dawn had come,
And fire and crones and wretchedness were gone.

# THE DENTIST

"This won't hurt a bit!"
The bland assurance shields the beast
Of highlighted malevolence,
Poised, loomed to take the feast.

Transposed, agape, and all aware—
Such frightful vulnerability.
I dare not move, rigid, affixed.
A prisoner in the dentist's chair!

Is this the succour that I seek,
The balm of pains that might have been?
Are digs and jabs I should not feel
Sad penance for a past unclean?

Such courage, such naivety;
I came and bared my soul to thee.
And in my fright, you watched me die
And revelled in the mastery.

So smile, but do not smile for me,
You subterfuge of sympathy.
For while my body cried with pain,
My eyes and heart are closed to thee!

# THE KING

I walked amongst the clouds
Until I came across a king
Surrounded by his followers,
Who whispered at the things
He pondered on as he looked down
Upon his world below.
He'd smile or frown as earth flew past
While rocking to and fro.

I walked across to meet him
Upon his cushioned sky.
I wondered whether he could see
My house as he went by.
The people all around him
Didn't like me being there,
But he just waved me to come to him
And stand beside his chair.

He knew all that I wanted
And pointed to the ground,
But it all looked the same to me
Upon his royal cloud.
The people all around us
Could only stand and stare,
As though they didn't understand
Why I should even care.

The king just smiled, but gently,
At my bewilderment,
Then waved his hands at all the world

Below his firmament.
"What you can see below, my child,
Are those who share or fight.
Yet what I see is what l know
As goodness and as strife."

I felt a little foolish
At such a silly task
As seeking out one little house
In such a scene so vast,
When all the worldly problems
That happen all the time
Are happiness or misery
To such a king as mine.

I'll wake up in the end, I'm sure,
And I sincerely hope
I'll still remember everything
Until I'm very old.

# THE PLOUGHMAN

The sweat of effort drifts like nectar through the grime of one more weary day.

Light, in its fading deception, plies aging shades of colour through images
Where stillness is the final word in this balmy evening play.

The signal pauses in this reflective montage are the contented snuffle
Of beasts pausing in tired contemplation on the release of their ties
And an occasional word of comfort.

Extending shadows reach out in searching skeins for places to rest and hide
With all the intrusive memories that only evenings in their silences can be privy to.

The plough lies in isolation, a discarded burden, sad companion
In its helplessness to the birds, which have pursued it throughout the day
With the desperation of mindful experience:

Now, perhaps they linger only because a farewell is due,
and companionships are deeper and needier than the wastes which are words.

Shudders are the song of chain and link as they sing of farewell
To the day and broadcast their liberation.

It's time to go home.

DANNY WARREN

# THEY'RE OFF!

Shuttered, sheltered, shuffling in a line,
Spring-loaded, barring snorting energy.
Uncounted eyes wait, eager for the blind
   Explosion of full-throated savagery.

A single, errant charger fights the goads
Before his gate, wild eyes disdaining all.
With calming, calling soothes, the beast is drawn,
   Persuaded, pushed, cajoled into its stall.

They're all set now as expectation mounts.
Brave, multicoloured riders wait, intense.
A crash, a burst, a cheering heady pound.
Dictated power careers towards the fence.

With bridled thunder, surging sweating hordes
Pelt neck and neck to cheering wild applause.

# THRUPPENNY BITS

Ah! Dear old thruppenny bits!
Symbol of much that vanished forever
On decimalstruction day.
All the optimism of a brave new hell
Was dashed in the first utterances
Of that fateful morning:
"Sorry, guv! We don't take thruppenny bits anymore.
Two and a half pees is the least that I can do now,
And that's the same as a tanner.
As for them half pees,
They're so small, aren't they?
I don't suppose I shall even be bothering with them
Before very long!"
I, on the other hand,
Have always cared for thruppenny bits.
You always knew where you were
With thruppenny bits.
Solid and recognisable, like life always was.
I suppose change is best for us,
Only having to count up to ten,
'Cause that's all the rest of the world can count up to.
It's just a shame that when we counted in bigger numbers,
Things always seemed to go that much further.
Then again,
As a nice politician once told me,
"Don't worry about your money, dear.
It'll always be the same.
Just remember!
None of this will ever affect the pound in your pocket."

# Time Being

Waken me, dear child,
Ere chance should wash my soul
In final memories,
And this poor state will leave me
Only painful recollections
Of past joys and sins.

Transcend regrets,
Mistaken harbour for this aching heart,
And let me see
Each instant of sad memory extolled.
Compressed in scenes as real
As liquid dream states,
Truth revealed.

For dreams are all
This dear existence, omnipresent,
Ever meant to be.
And timeless effort, seemingly eternal,
Blends its history
Into the substance of my total being,
Then fades from me.

# TOBACCO ROAD

Love taste never quite goes away.
Love affair,
But like the holder,
The need,
The craving.
How do we all manage it?
Basking in the residue of disposed discharge:
Unwanted residue,
The smirks of undisguised satisfaction.
I do envy them their pleasure.
God knows I've claimed them for myself often enough,
Stopping and starting,
Always thinking that I could stop again
Whenever I chose to,
And then finding that I couldn't.
Waiting until the right moment came,
When I could
Stop again,
Then start again.
It's over now for good.
But in my heart of hearts, I wish it wasn't.

# TODAY

Attending change and charmless misery,
Hawked as feisty lies, this bold new age
Of expectation and regret, too close to be
A true perspective to this helpless sage.

Brave promises are sugar-coated fairy tales
Of blessings that are served as daily life
With smiles and salutations, easy time entails
Disposal of all trouble and all strife.

In helplessness, I languish in my sad regrets,
Consumed by an electrifying state
Of blissfully inert, remotely handheld sets
That serve up all existence on a plate.

But would I hold a candle to a lesser time
If shaded in its comfort I could laze benign?

# TOLLESBURY TIDES

Chimes that rattle in the rigging
Call the early birds to prayer:
Stifled Latin chants, the sighing
Wind that hastens stormy air.

Guided home by expectations
Of a morning, of a song:
Stuka'd screams cavort and battle
Time till timelessness is gone.

Interruption gently scudded
Laziness befitting times
Eloquence in rivulets:
Gently chasing ripple rhymes.

Proudly nonchalant, he idles,
All his world and all his care
In the comfort of a knowledge
Generations smile and share.

Salt marsh sailor, seemly silent
In the bosom of the bay,
Balmed within the gentle swaying
Of a prayerful holiday:

I could join you if you'd let me,
Sing with you a deeper song
In the silence of a breathless
Waking prayer to Tollesbury young.

# TOO LATE

Regret still lives in memory compressed
Of youthful hop, the local Mecca scene:
When wanton times restrained by awkwardness
Meant foolish hesitations intervened.

With wild devotion, blatant bodies called
Their invitation notice to the crowd
Of seemingly disinterested boys,
Dispersed in groups, engaged in chatter loud.

If unity is strength, so did I sin:
Some need to be as different as the rest,
Foreswore my natural desire to win
The heart that called me out with eyed caress.

If folly lies in rueing thought the most,
What price forsaken loves forsaken ghosts.

# TREE FELLERS

Dear matriarchal coexistent,
Evergladed, mystic super scene.
What tears you keep
Of seeping bark
And weeping evergreen.
How can you know
That soulnessness of alien,
Intrusive infamy,
With cheerful carelessness,
Will rip thy very soul
Away from thee?

And can it be
That quiet stillness,
Peace, tranquillity
Will fade in leaden silences
Of mystery
And faithful benefactors,
Friends so dear to thee
Of bark and bough,
Will reach into the sky
For frantic liberty?

And now you lie,
Prostrate and forest floored
Amid your scattered seed;
Rejuvenated offspring,
Waking to survival's greed,
To seek relinquished life
And flee the tranquil gloom
Where star and sky are feast days
In this wooded womb.

DANNY WARREN

# TRUST

See a truth and share a lie.
Unburden your misery.
I could tell you with a smile
How easy pain unbared may be.
Should I tolerate your story
In the twinkling of your eyes,
Dressed up in such vagaries—
Sincerity in disguise?
Truth and lies! Ah, what's the difference
In the end and in the way
That I love you in your mischief,
Dearest lover, every day!

# TWILIGHT

Lapping wavelets chatter on the shore,
Exhausted by the efforts of the day,
To fall and foam in idle rivulets
Of anxious life and gentle interplay.

The soft surf hums the gently chorused foam
In lulling whispered solitude and care,
To bathe in sunlight, resting in farewells
Of sad seas calming sheen and evening air.

The silent day is restless in its calm,
As seabirds search the brightly silvered shore
In purposeful observance of the day:
To nod and dance in glorious encore.

As even time brings subtle alchemy,
So night-time's cloak embraces mysteries.

# UNEMPLOYMENT

Empty parking spaces.
Empty, nervous faces.
Gloom pervades this scene of shattered dreams.
Thoughts so self-contained,
So secretive, restrained,
Speak volumes for the waste of might-have-beens.

All those brave new worlds,
All those dreams unfurled,
Lie dying for a mean, unwelcome phrase.
Fearful thoughts condemn
These melancholy men
To insecurity and lonely days.

Praise these lonely times
Of liberty and crime,
As real employment lies in disarray,
And job security,
The final fallacy,
Is friendless arbiter of life's malaise.

# VOCAL MIRROR

Vocal mirror, do I know you?
Echo of a stranger me.
Less than comfortable reminder
Of a self I never see.
Audio and visual
Mirror of an imagery
Evident to this poor body's
Quaint familiarities.

# Waking Dreams

Asleep, awake.
Sleep wakes endless journey
Through subliminal existences
And onward to nowhere.

Time, not here,
Not in this place where all is now,
And all just seems to be,
Then disappear.

Yet there are times
I see you as you are,
Beneath the veil of rational perception,
Of pure imagination,
In random flow.
And then who knows
Whether I'll choose to stay a while,
Or go.

# WALL ART

Do I enjoy wall art?
All the best vandals of prehistory did it,
And it didn't do the causes that they espoused—
Too much harm at the end of the day.
Colours are better today,
Brighter, brasher, braver,
With perhaps a shade too much angst for my taste,
As well as being a little too short on storyline.

Do I enjoy wall art?
Symmetrical brick design, while neat in its own way,
Doesn't really lend itself
To what I like to think of as imaginative stimuli.
Words float in lurid sparks,
Lost in a blaze of vivid arrogance
To seekers of understanding.
Maybe an expression
Of the right to deface,
Rather than a need to say anything
Of importance!

Do I enjoy wall art?
Not as much as children, it seems,
Confusing what they say
With what they play.
Walls need it like a coat of careful introspection.
Maybe it's just as well
That wall art won't outlive the space that it fills.
Truth will be wherever I can find it,
But having it bawled at me in lurid cacophonies
Means it loses its message
In the end.

# WAR

Demon beast, plenipotential
Conscious travesty.
Seed ignominy still,
We freely welcome thee.
Sad blindness yet, we draw our strength;
Insane hypocrisy:
Safe knowledge in our Mother Earth,
We live and die in thee.

Good plaudits and refrains we share
With those who won and lost.
The cries for half-brave heroes
Left alone to weigh the cost.
What peace was it that left them there,
To wonder at their sin?
Sad questions from the soul of man
For them to suffer in.

So children, in your joy and pain,
Remember who it was,
Invoked the cries for peace
And said there had to be a cause.
Then ask them if the time has come
To find another way
To shape the course humanity
Should take to judgement day.

# WAR

You cruel deceiver, still you play
Your music for the soul of man.
Brave promises in sweetened spells
Entice with lie and heady plan.

Excitement; celebrated cause
Does curse with true sincerity,
All cruelty and wickedness,
Belligerent humanity.

So eager and so willingly
You rally to the cry,
Till bravery and ignorance
Leave you awaking as you die.

DANNY WARREN

# D'EAU

Do I disturb you,
Highlighting the accompaniments
Of sterile oblivion?
I share time with you
And continue,
Aware only of moment,
And space,
And being.
All existence is,
And all I may do, is traverse you,
As aware of it
As it is of me.
As you are of me,
I am to you,
And that is all
And everything.
Ah! The things I've seen,
If only I could remember.
I am aloft, afloat,
And cold,
And alone,
And earth is in me.

# WATER

Tell me in your own good time
About my purpose at life and death.
Wasted away on tides of memory
To squander diluted nightmares
For the lies which are my purity.
I should be excused for the sake of my stories
As you feed and become me,
Adding your small part
To the sins and the sanctity
Of surreal confusion.
I dance on winds of wonder,
Making the world my own,
Carrying the infection of pain
To the corners which I make mine
As I love and am loved
In the name of life.

# WHY NOT

Misshapen concepts plague the vast divide
Between the great distributor of sins
And all the good intentions cast aside
That gave existence meaning to my dreams.

Still, take my hand and lead me by my soul
Through mischief minefields, scatter rugs of play,
For all the world as if the lie of gold
Was true perception visiting each day.

And if in pause, I question what I do
To ease the painful legacy that age,
With cultivated doubt, has misconstrued,
Will disappointment share this centre stage?

If love is lacked when love of life is killed,
Still life is stilled when life is unfulfilled.

# WISH

Wishful thinking, wish me well
That I might bathe in blossoms' bell:
So sweet that all the dreams I heed
Should please this sense and sense this plea.

I wish for all the world as if
A wish alone were lasting bliss
And twilights of forgetfulness
Are morning's sensitive caress.

Ah! Star-borne messenger at play,
Your fiery message mends the day
With gathered instant hopes and dreams,
And swift displays of fiery beams.

DANNY WARREN

# WOODLAND WALK

Trees whisper their welcome
With mysterious songs of breathless silences.
The calm indifference of a dying day
Fades with the ebbing light of one more play,
Then begs me stay.

The shadowy rustle of some dark secret
Warns of the alien kindness,
Which is the caress of reassurance
Dispelling forever the terrors of childhood,
Daring my fear.

Dusk and sleep enfold the life
Of benevolent fellowship and death.
Intrusive trepidation lurks in the sultry shadow
Of a moon which bathes its own
In the restlessness of cruel existence,
Yet leads me to home.

# WORDS

Eyes!
Passing, meeting;
Fleeting greeting;
Knowing!
Such brief instances
Of brilliant comprehension,
Such language,
Such completeness!

Oh! sad suspicion,
To doubt your true integrity
Is my innate deceit;
It gives me pause
To see what can't be hidden,
To be what really is!

Nakedness
Shielded with words,
Lest some perception
Of the inner soul.
My secret being,
Be discovered, unlovered;
Laid bare before
My telepathic eyes!

Still seeking,
Hoping against hope!
That look
Belies the inconsistency
Of my own doubts,

DANNY WARREN

Nurturing a vague conviction
That all I ever needed to know
Is laid inside my bared soul.
And words are just confusion,
After all!

# YOUTH

I could have been what you wanted,
If I had lied about all the things
That you said were important.

I could even have presumed on your naivety
And smiled for your satisfaction
And your soul.

How much did I want to be the person
I thought you wanted me to be?
Did it work for you?

Didn't you see through the sham
That you yourself have been party to
For most of your own life?

In the accepted scheme of things,
I can only construe my life in terms
That register failures.

Suffer me in silence
While I dwell on the misery of that place
And cry alone.

# A Zealot's Prayer

Distance yourself from all shame
And all disgrace.
My death is in the well of tears,
Drowning in the ministries
Of intolerance.
Uneasy laughter regales our fears
With the distraction of blame
And recrimination.
Nation speaks peace unto nation
With downcast desperation,
The laurel and the gun
Making an uneasy alliance.
For more and for less
Is death the prize
And the leveller of all promises.
For I who have nothing
Have nothing to give but myself.

# ABOUT THE AUTHOR

I am merely a glimmer in this maelstrom of existence. I lived a life of choices which were imposed on me but which were not mine to make. I lacked the benefits of parenthood, growing instead in an altogether more regulated regime of rigid stability. Love of language and Shakespeare has always existed; certainly for as long as I can remember and I never minded being described as a voracious reader. Many were the occasions when I would plead with the teacher to persue some aspect of a particular english lesson to the chagrin of my classmates. For many years I have dabbled in the arts as well as in poetry more with the reading than with the writing and this collection is simply an amalgam of random expressions which were the result of life events stimulated by emotional reactions and responses: Then I would put pen to paper. They include some sonnets and many free verse poems which I have a particular liking for. I have always felt the need to involve the vast majority of society in my stories even if they are not even aware that any difficulties exist. It was perhaps fortunate that I lacked the benefits of a normal family upbringing: It did mean that the path which I chose through my life was divined more by my sad instincts for survival at the time as well as the rigorous directions which popular media insisted that I should follow. Living with nuns would have been more of an eye opener if I had had a yardstick to judge them by: As it was, they were my life and my controllers throughout my childhood until I was released without preparation or warning into a world full of painful contradictions. I never understood the confusion of unexpected rejections and unkindnesses with which I had to deal.

Cest le vie!

For Marian. But for you this book would not have happened.

Lightning Source UK Ltd.
Milton Keynes UK
UKOW03n1423230317

297372UK00001B/15/P